CAT[...]IM
A

Marshall Cavendish Editions

© 2017 Catherine Lim

Cover design by Lorraine Aw
Photo of woman by Hisu Lee (unsplash.com)

First published 2003 by Horizon Books

This edition published 2017 by Marshall Cavendish Editions
An imprint of Marshall Cavendish International

A member of the
Times Publishing Group

All rights reserved

No part of this publication may be reproduced, stored in a retrieval system or
transmitted, in any form or by any means, electronic, mechanical, photocopying,
recording or otherwise, without the prior permission of the copyright owner.
Requests for permission should be addressed to the Publisher, Marshall Cavendish
International (Asia) Private Limited, 1 New Industrial Road, Singapore 536196.
Tel: (65) 6213 9300.
E-mail: genref@sg.marshallcavendish.com
Website: www.marshallcavendish.com/genref

The publisher makes no representation or warranties with respect to the contents
of this book, and specifically disclaims any implied warranties or merchantability
or fitness for any particular purpose, and shall in no event be liable for any loss
of profit or any other commercial damage, including but not limited to special,
incidental, consequential, or other damages.

Other Marshall Cavendish Offices:
Marshall Cavendish Corporation. 99 White Plains Road, Tarrytown NY 10591-
9001, USA • Marshall Cavendish International (Thailand) Co Ltd. 253 Asoke,
12th Flr, Sukhumvit 21 Road, Klongtoey Nua, Wattana, Bangkok 10110, Thailand
• Marshall Cavendish (Malaysia) Sdn Bhd, Times Subang, Lot 46, Subang Hi-Tech
Industrial Park, Batu Tiga, 40000 Shah Alam, Selangor Darul Ehsan, Malaysia

Marshall Cavendish is a registered trademark of Times Publishing Limited

National Library Board, Singapore Cataloguing-in-Publication Data

Name(s): Lim, Catherine.
Title: A leap of love / Catherine Lim.
Description: Singapore : Marshall Cavendish Editions, [2017] | Originally
published by Horizon Books Pte Ltd, 2003.
Identifier(s): OCN 988916017 | ISBN 978-981-4779-56-2 (paperback)
Subject(s): First loves--Fiction. | Man-woman relationships--Fiction.
Classification: DDC S823--dc23

Printed in Singapore by JCS Digital Solutions Pte Ltd

One

Chang Li-Ann, undergraduate of the University of Singapore in 1980, wrote, in the middle of a boring lecture, a love poem to an as yet non-existent lover. She wrote with feverish energy, the tip of a pink tongue curled against upper lip, a swatch of hair fallen over one shoulder, unaware that watching her, were four pairs of eyes belonging to four already existing lovers – if only she would allow them that role.

The pen, gripped firmly, glided effortlessly.

One of the hopeful young men who always went through an elaborate pretence of looking for a seat in the vast, seldom filled lecture theatre, his eyes tightly narrowed in earnest, frowning search, before alighting, with a great show of surprise, on the seat next to Li-ann's, now made the mistake of craning his neck to peep at the mysterious words flowing so smoothly from her pen. He withdrew instantly, stung by a cold look and an angry hand slammed protectively over the writing.

For all his ardent admiration of her, the poor young man's existence went entirely unnoticed, except when it obtruded on hers, as so many stares to be averted, so many unwelcome offers of favours to be instantly declined. Undaunted, the poor young man whose name was Raymond Tan Sin Liang, watched, hid, followed. Once, he had left a bouquet of roses outside the door of her hostel room, with a card of effusive declaration tucked among the blooms. He had very foolishly decided, in a sudden access of bashfulness, to hide the elegantly beribboned roses under a huge mess of old newspapers.

Li-ann had stepped over them when she returned, and the cleaning woman had later swept them into her dust-pan.

Raymond Tan Sin Liang, after the unfortunate incident of the roses, began to look elsewhere, his ardour by no means diminished, stoically smiling through varying degrees of female rejection. Then in 1983, the year of his graduation, he was finally rewarded. She was a graduate from a polytechnic, pretty enough and not fastidious as to looks or social finesse in a partner. Above all, she loved him for himself. To her, Raymond could now give, in full measure, the love of his simple, generous heart. He became a very happy man.

But that would be 1983, still three years away. Now that honest heart found no takers.

The boring lecturer droned on, and Li-ann wrote on, now and again casting a suspicious glance at the intrusive peeper. She wrote defiantly and breathed life into a dream. Hitherto only an abstraction in the golden nimbus of her imagination where he had been sold resident for the past year, the dream now tumbled upon the solid back of a brown, used envelope, and acquired a habitation and a name.

She decided that like her, he was born and brought up in Singapore. Like hers, his name bore the chic hyphen. Wu-er – she still did not know what he looked like – was the sole recipient of all the love and longing that her young, ardent heart was capable of.

She wrote:

"There is a place I want to go to, but I don't know where
There is someone I want to meet, but I don't know who."

Hers was a love, nurtured to fullness, in search of a lover. She had to fall in love with love, before she could fall in love with a person.

She knew now. The place did not have to be Singapore. The name did not have to be Wu-er. These were only playful games of the imagination that she allowed herself while she waited. Playfulness, it was said, was the lover's special claim and privilege. All lovers, in their joy, became children again. For the present, she would be playful on her own. When HE appeared at last, he whose name could only be designated by the exalted capital letters of breathless worship, she would have a partner in love's laughing innocence.

When would he appear? She would know, with a certainty of the heart that surpassed any understanding by the mind, inferior organ by far, in the eternal human quest. She would know when place and person came together in the moment of love's epiphany. The road to love's Damascus had its blinding lights too: she would be dazzled for one moment, then get up, rub her eyes and come face to face with the promised presence waiting at the end of the road.

"This is the greatest nonsense I've ever heard," said her mother who had been very anxiously looking for a good match for her very pretty, very intelligent daughter from her seventeenth birthday. Now approaching twenty two, Li-ann was in danger of the worst fate that could befall women – spinsterhood. Mrs Chang's loving, motherly heart suffered severe palpitations at that horrible prospect.

She stood before Li-ann and raised her left hand to show five outspread fingers, each representing a missed marriage opportunity, each hence a bitter maternal disappointment. With the forefinger of her right hand, she systematically went through each of the five big fish that her daughter, foolish, headstrong girl that she was, had allowed to get away.

One, the youngest son of a High Court judge; two, the economics graduate who was a President's Scholar; three, the son of the business tycoon T.C. Khor who was a bit of a playboy but would surely settle into the contentment of domesticity after marriage; four, Terence Yong who came from a poor family but was holding a high-salaried job in an international finance company; five, Richard Low who had all the makings of a good husband and provider, though he was a little overweight, and not as good-looking as the rest.

They had all come courting, had all been allowed a date or two and then consigned to oblivion. After each date, as soon as the ·car roared away into the night, Mrs Chang, in pyjamas and curlers, appeared, followed her daughter to her room, watched her kick off her shoes and unzip her dress and said, "So?"

Li-ann who had a perverse pleasure in teasing her mother and watching her dilate her eyes or throw up her hands in horror said, "Mother, don't you understand? He cannot pronounce the 'r' sound and he begins each sentence with 'I understands…'"

Mrs Chang said severely, "Young lady, don't you act stuck-up!" Her daughter allowed something as trivial as English grammar to negate the value of a high-paying job, a good family background, a totally dependable moral character.

Li-ann said, "It's no use, Mother. I keep telling you, but you won't listen. HE's already there, waiting for me."

An absurd figment of girlish fancy standing between spinsterhood and fulfilment, between stigma and prestige! Mrs Chang grimaced and twirled a forefinger against the side of her head, to signal the onset of madness in her daughter. But there was a glimmer of hope in her eyes when she asked, "What about K.S.?"

K.S. came far below any of the five, since he had no car and lived in: a small, government-subsidised flat with his parents and sister. But Li-ann seemed to like him. She had seen them laughing together. She had peeped, in her pyjamas and curlers, and seen them holding hands on the sofa. K.S. could be the last hope against a husbandless future.

Li-ann said, "My heart says, 'No, not him.'"

"Heart! Heart! Why don't you listen to your head for once? In a few years' time you'll be twenty five!" cried Mrs Chang in exasperation, twenty five being the age for the alarm bells to start ringing shrilly.

She decided to resort to a shrewd maternal strategy that was known to have worked well: "Look at all your friends. They have boyfriends already. You are the only one left out." She held out the bleak prospect and watched her daughter's reaction. Li-ann was unmoved.

She resorted to a final, desperate strategy. Her eyes suddenly filling with tears, she said, "Who will take care of you when I'm gone?" Li-ann remained unmoved and went on to brush her hair and get ready for bed.

She liked K. S. He had that something that the others lacked, a refreshing air of nonchalance, an ability not to take himself too seriously. Perhaps that was a cover for the depth of his feeling. He called frequently. "So?" he would say, going straight to the point. It was amazing how into that single monosyllable a mother could squeeze so much reproach, an aspiring lover so much hope.

Her own language for repudiation was less terse: "Oh, K.S.,

you know I can't. I've already explained things to you."

No aspiring lover, facing the beloved in the solidity of flesh and blood, likes to be outdone by a rival not yet in existence. He hid his vexation in childish play, taking out an imaginary knife to slit, with a flourish, the throat of the imaginary rival.

K.S. said, with the bright gleam of sudden understanding, "I think I know what it's all about. You've been for too long on a diet of romantic literature where love's fulfilment is actually its unattainability. All those brooding, sullen heroes of Victorian novels that you girls swoon over, standing tall and upright out there upon a wild heath in a wild storm, out of reach. I bet you have devoured hundreds of these novels." He watched for her reaction. There was a suppressed amusement which animated her features and made her look so beautiful his heart ached. But he went on with the spirited accusation. He got bolder. "Hey, rid yourself of those false dreams. If I were a surgeon, I'd recommend an illusionectomy."

She threw a cushion at him. He threw it back, and was upon her in an instant, his face very close, except that she moved hers aside swiftly, so that once again, he missed the opportunity for the first kiss.

She laughed. Now she knew why she liked him. He had such a wonderful way with language, such a delightfully refreshing way of expressing his feelings, whether of annoyance or longing.

She liked K.S. very much. But he claimed no part of her heart. It was a heart rich and abundant, ready for the claiming, and the claimant stood somewhere along the path Fate was leading her. At some point, Fate, ever a gentle, benign presence, would stop, bend down and whisper, "That's HIM," closing the first chapter of ardent search and opening the next one of joyous meeting, discovery and fulfilment.

Two

Don't believe this," said Li-ann. "Resorting to a fortune-teller, in my desperation to find a man."

The desperation was actually her mother's. Mrs Chang had come home one afternoon excitedly exclaiming, "Fantastic! The name, the age, even the mole on the right cheek! And she doesn't accept any money, only a donation to her temple. Imagine predicting the mole! And she can walk everywhere without help."

Slowly, patiently, Li-ann pieced together the story. One of her mother's mahjong friends, Mrs Khoo, had discovered an old, totally blind woman living in the Cheng Si Tok Temple, who had the uncanny ability not only to find her way around unaided, but also to look into the future. Her gift moreover took on the dear focus of a specialisation, choosing to be at the service only of unhappy young women in search of husbands. It dedicated itself to love alone, and scorned to be used for men and women in search of health or that coveted prize in the Grand Singapore Lottery every month.

An old, blind woman, approaching ninety, who had never married and would die a virgin, held young women's soft trembling hands in her old, gnarled ones, and warmed their hearts with hope. There were rumours that she had been a very beautiful girl in a small village in China, had become blind under the most cruel circumstances, and then awakened one morning to find the gift.

She had told Mrs Khoo's twenty-six-year-old daughter that she would meet a man soon, describing him in detail. Mrs Khoo said that when her Rosie was introduced to Albert recently at a dinner party, she almost fainted upon sight of the mole on the right cheek. They had been dating since.

Mrs Chang said firmly to Li-ann, "Tomorrow we go together to the Cheng Si Tok Temple. I've got an *ang pow* ready," the cash donation being a substantial one, in keeping with her generosity.

Li-ann affected a massive indifference that hid an overpowering curiosity. She had heard that one in three women in Singapore had, at one time or other, consulted a fortune teller about love or marriage, on behalf of daughters, sisters, best friends or themselves. With her dream securely locked in her heart, she would offer herself with amused detachment, as one more statistic.

She had three good friends at the university with whom she shared her secrets.

"Well?" they asked. "Did the blind one tell you when you will meet your dream man? Does he have a mole on his cheek? Or any unobservable part of the dream physique?"

They were inclined to be irreverent. They all had boyfriends and dated furiously.

"Nothing," said Li-ann. "She took my hands and began to talk rapidly. It sounded like a lot of gibberish to me. I didn't understand the dialect. Mother did and was upset. We left quickly."

It had been a strange morning indeed. Mrs Chang, hoping to hear good news, saw the old blind woman suddenly drop her daughter's hands and begin to sway from side to side on her small, wooden stool, shaking her head and making strange little sounds. Mrs Chang watched for a while, in growing alarm, then decided to drag her daughter away, but not before pressing the *ang pow* into the old one's hands.

"Well, what did she say?" Li-ann had asked. Her mother became evasive.

"Nothing, nothing," she cried. "Don't tell anyone." "But what did she say?" Li-ann persisted.

This time her mother was angry. "It's Mrs Khoo's fault. She should have been clearer about something she told me. It seems the old one sometimes gets into strange moods and can't tell fortunes. Or tells them all wrong. Mrs Khoo should have informed me properly."

"Mother, I still want you to tell me what the fortune-teller said."

"Something about pain and fire," said Mrs Chang slowly, in an awe-stricken voice. But turning to her daughter and vigorously fanning her body with both hands to disperse any malodorous airs that might still be clinging to it from that very regrettable visit, she said, with a final show of great casualness, "don't think about it anymore. And don't tell anyone." Neither had spoken of the incident since.

"'Pain and fire,'" repeated Kim, the closest of the three friends. "She means you'll have to go through all the tortures of love's true path, which never runs smooth, you know."

Li-ann pitied her friends. For they could not love, or chose not to love with joyous and complete abandon. In moments of honesty, they qualified their love for their boyfriends with so many 'buts' and 'ifs', hateful words that should have no place in love's vocabulary.

Kim said, "I love Soong but…", meaning that she was aware of all his shortcomings, including a tendency towards childish, selfish behaviour, and the non-possession of a car which sometimes caused inconvenience in their dates. But he was better than no one; she had been so lonely since she broke up with Lawrence.

Suneetha who was even more forthcoming with her secrets, said, "I'll give all my love to Sanjay if…" The conditional had something to do with his meekness in the presence of his formidable mother who dictated the colour of his shirts and ties, paced the floor with angry energy if he came back late from a date, and reduced his girlfriends to tears.

"Then why are you still dating him?" demanded Li-ann.

"I don't know," said Suneetha miserably.

She did know. If Patrick, someone she had met in London a year ago, flew back to Singapore, appeared on her doorstep and said, "I've decided to take a job here after all. For your sake," she would instantly call Sanjay, write him a kind but firm note, or simply ignore his calls until he got the message and stayed away. Goodbye to all that. It would be so easy.

But it was Jennie who went the whole way of brutal honesty.

"You want to know how much I love Julian? As much as he loves me, no more no less. Last week was more, this week is going to be a little less. You want to know for how long? Until I meet someone better. Then it's bye bye! Don't be shocked. He's planning the same move. I know. It's all a game."

Jennie reduced love to a transaction of exact reciprocity – so much from you, hence this much from me. Worse, she made lovers look like two sleek-shanked animals tensely, warily circling each other, waiting for the next move.

Kim, Suneetha, Jennie – they squandered their love uselessly while waiting for the right one to come along. Soong, Sanjay, Julian – they were only lovers by default, lovers in transit, the pitiful consolation prize in love's grand lottery.

It was horrible, the purity of this marvel called love debased by the crude calculations of an abacus clicking away in the brain. She saw Kim, Suneetha and Jennie, three pretty maids in a row, their arms folded across their chests, their brows deeply knit, their eyes tightly narrowed, in a mental concentration on love's algorithms of cost and benefit.

She would never allow the tiniest crack, the smallest stain in her love's crystal.

Now it was the turn of the three friends to attack her. They said, "Why are you so sure you will meet your Mr Right, your knight in shining armour on the white charger?"

She winced at the banality of the allusions, Mr Right suggesting the caricature of comic books, the knight in armour the trite imagery of cheap romantic fiction. HE was simply 'The Promised One', promised by Fate who had peeped into her heart and understood its yearnings ever since, at the age of twelve, she had looked scornfully at the gawky, immature boys around her and swore she would never get married, and at twenty had decided she wanted to get married after all , but in the way her heart wanted. Thereafter she had embarked on her secret dream. She made a bargain with Fate; Fate would deliver.

"Even if you met such a person, how would you know it was HIM?" Her answer irritated them to the point of exasperation. The heart knows. The heart does. The heart simply is.

What sort of answer was that? They threw up their hands at the outrageous illogicality of it all. Li-ann, one of the most promising students in the Final Year Arts course was unbelievably irrational when it came to love and marriage.

They would not let go, and persisted with their questions, determined to drag her out of her irrationality.

"Even if you knew it was HIM, how could you be sure that he would return your love?"

Now it was his heart. His heart would know. It would know instantaneously and respond, in full measure.

The absurd girl had reduced love's long arduous process of meeting and discovery, evaluation and adjustment, deliberation and decision, to one blinding apocalyptic moment. There was nothing more to ask or say. They threw up their hands once more.

"Well good luck to you, you incurable romantic, and to that super, know-all organ of yours. Tell us when the golden clouds in the sky part and he descends to a blare of trumpets, when the white charger comes thundering up!" said the three pragmatic women. They laughed and went back to their imperfect loves in an imperfect world.

It happened exactly a week later, as she was walking along busy Orchard Road. There were no golden parting clouds, only thick billows of grey smoke from a thundering lorry, that cleared to show him sitting at a table in a small corner open-air café ambitiously called 'Blue Paradise'. He was reading a book and drinking coffee.

She stopped, caught her breath and stared. It would only be later that she could explain the sudden stopping, right in the midst of angrily honking cars.

"I was going to turn into Hong Keng Road to do an errand for my mother, when the whisper came at last. 'Stop,' it said. I stopped and there he was."

Through whizzing vehicles and hurrying pedestrians, she caught sight of a blue denim shirt, grey cotton pants. Neat glasses. A neat haircut. A flick of hair tumbling over the forehead and a strong hand moving swiftly up to push it back. A moment of looking up from the engrossing book to take out a white handkerchief to wipe the glasses and put them back on. A luminous dream that had come to earth as a concrete name on the back of a used envelope was enlarging before her very eyes into a solid corporeal presence in a roadside café.

"Go on," said the whisper, and suffused her whole being with a tremulous joy. "What are you waiting for?"

Three

She had to act quickly. That solid presence, in the denim shirt and cotton pants, sitting on a brown wooden chair by a round, marble-topped table in a café, might just evaporate in a moment – poof! – and then Fate would turn to her reproachfully and say, "I've done my part; why didn't you do yours?"

In all the fairy tales of her childhood, the chance for lifelong fortune or happiness hung tremblingly upon one split second action: uncorking that genie-bottle pulled up from the ocean depths, cracking open that ancient witch-tree with one precise swing of the rescuing axe, pressing one's lips upon the face of that uncomely toad to bring him forth into princely resplendence.

She would have to do something fast, or Fate would take away that once-in-a-lifetime, once-upon-a-tremulous moment chance. But no, the Fate that had been her co conspirator for years now, was gentle, not severe, generous, not exacting. She could almost see this benign presence smiling at her. She stood spellbound and watched, from the opposite side of the road, her dream now securely contained in a body and performing the reassuringly earthbound function of drinking coffee. She craned her neck, twisted her body and jumped up and down in a frantic effort to obtain a complete view of the Promised One, fractured by a hundred interposing lorries, buses and cars. Now she could see three quarters of the face, now only part of the hand holding the book, the next moment the entire book with a few words of the title clearly visible.

A delivery van – horror of horrors! – parked itself in front of the café, and blocked out the vision completely. She made impatient little sounds, and waved an impatient hand, to shoo away the annoying obstruction, but it stayed, for a full minute, before roaring away. She heaved a sigh of relief. He was still there, thank goodness, solid as ever, drinking his coffee, totally absorbed in his book.

She saw a young woman approaching him, and saw him look up with a smile. The sight was unwelcome, to say the least. She felt a twinge of something like real jealousy, hating competition, in any form, to any extent, even at this very incipient stage.

She saw them smiling at each other and frowned. He stood up as if to move towards the woman, and she bit her lip in vexation. Hateful presence, obtruding upon her dream! Then her face cleared in the brightness of understanding and relief The young woman was only a stranger, an irrelevance. She had apparently come to ask if she could have one of the unoccupied chairs at his table, and he had apparently not only said yes but offered to carry it to her table for her. She watched a little tableau of gallantry and laughing refusal, and then the young woman was gone, lugging away the chair herself, and leaving him to continue with the reading and the coffee.

She looked around wildly for inspiration. The manner of her approach of him, in those few precious moments allowed by Fate – who could tell when he would get up, pay the bill, leave the café, mingle with the crowd outside and be lost forever to her? – had to be something inspired and inspiring, worthy of the best traditions of romantic first encounters. The opening chapter had to throb to the beat of love's vibrant, inventive powers. None of that prosaic quality of the familiar self-introduction: "Hi, I'm Li-ann. May I...", accompanied by the inevitable fear of polite rejection: "I'm sorry. I'm leaving in a moment," or "I'm sorry, this seat's taken." No, she would, now that the dream had begun to unfold, take it on a rising trajectory of breathless development. Inspiration – she needed inspiration.

The heart, in conspiracy with an ever friendly Fate said, "Look to your right, near the bus-stop." She looked to the right, near the bus-stop, and saw a stall selling newspapers, actually only a rough wooden trestle, presided over by a stout, bald-headed Indian man in a singlet, and a small, skinny boy in an oversized T-shirt, presumably his son, earnestly counting coins in his hands. There was a signboard in front that announced the date for that day: 29 February 1980.

All her romantic instincts, galvanised for action, had been directed to a mundane signboard, one of many dotting the busy roads in Singapore, giving mundane information of the date for the day. The date, in bold black print, announcing the last day of a uniquely appointed month in civilisation's calendar, danced before her eyes in the bright late morning sunshine.

"Oh my god – of course," breathed Li-ann, in a sudden burst of understanding. "Why didn't I see it earlier...", and instantly swung into action.

She rushed to the stall and bought a newspaper for the sole purpose of folding it tightly to use as a pad on which to write something. On a piece of notepaper hurriedly torn from a notebook in her handbag, she wrote, in her neat handwriting:

"'There is a place want to go to, but I don't know where
There is someone I want to meet but I don't know who.'

Place and person have come together! Right here in Orchard Road at" (looking at her watch) "11.38 a.m. I'm taking advantage of the opportunity granted by universal tradition to us females only on 29 February – imagine, only once every four years – to approach the males of our desire with requests that they cannot turn down. This special day allows us to make a leap of love! Watch out! Note the sanctity of the enjoinder upon you males – you cannot say No. So here's my request, elevated to a command by this noblest of traditions: Meet me at the same café, same table, at eight o'clock this evening. You can't see me, but I'm going to watch your every movement very closely!"

With trembling fingers, she folded up the piece of paper. Then she approached the small skinny boy at the news-stand, stretching out a palm to display a scattering of coins which made his large, bright eyes gleam. "All yours," she said, "if you take this letter to that gentleman sitting at that table over there."

The small boy, as soon as he understood, looked up at his father for a nod of approval, then scooped the coins into his own palm, took the letter and was off. His lithe body wove in and out of the traffic, like some small, agile animal. She watched him put the letter in the gentleman's hands, and was glad that when the small boy pointed in her direction, clearly in response to his queries, both looked to see nobody. For she had adroitly slipped away and was now among a group of shoppers in a clothing store four doors away, a good vantage position to watch whatever would unfold.

It unfolded rapidly, as if set in unstoppable motion by the daringly inspired note. Partially hidden by two large women examining a variety of blouses, she watched him open the note and read it. She wanted to see every nuance of expression on his face, as his eyes moved through the closely-written lines exploding in their lethal mix of confession, longing and challenge. If only those wretched vehicles would stop whizzing by! But she managed to catch a lot – a quizzical frown, a tiny smile playing around the corners of his mouth, that expanded into a broad grin as he folded up the letter and got up briskly from his seat. He was moving very quickly and purposefully, as if ready, on his part, to swing into decisive action.

She watched him weave his way quickly past several tables, to the back of the café, where he suddenly stopped. He stood facing a young woman in a pink gingham dress, clearly one of the café waitresses, and appeared to be talking to her in an animated way.

Li-ann watched with an intensity that she tried to disguise by pretending to show the same interest in the blouses as the two women shoppers. His back was turned towards her, so she could not see the expression on his face. With her note in his hand, he seemed to be talking with great earnestness. Why on earth would he be telling a waitress about a mysterious note he had received on the special day of 29 February? Unless, of course, he knew her well. Perhaps she was a close friend, a girlfriend even. For the second time, Li-ann felt an upsurge of jealousy; it rose from somewhere deep inside and coated throat and tongue with the bitterness of something very like fear.

She moved to the front of the shop, to get a closer view. She saw the waitress throw back her head and laugh, saw him turn his head briefly and caught sight of a laughing profile. And now she felt angry and humiliated. They were making fun of her! Or rather, of the besotted writer of the note, whoever she was. It made not the slightest difference to her that they would never know the writer's identity.

Li-ann felt a searing flush spread across her cheeks and

her neck; it was as if that note, so full of the joyful, innocent insouciance of lovers' play, had been crushed into a nasty little ball and flung back at her.

A bus once more blocked her view. It moved slowly, far too slowly, for it gave him time to disappear from her sight. He was no longer in the café.

And then she gave a gasp and clutched at her throat in a paroxysm of shock, wonder and joy. He was standing on the road in front of the café, in the midst of noisily honking vehicles and staring pedestrians, his legs apart and planted firmly on the ground, his arms raised high over his head, hands outspread and palms turned outwards, the right palm bearing the large letter 'O', and the left one 'K', scrawled with something that looked like red chalk or paint. He was swaying from side to side, so that the letters, like missing items from a child's alphabet set that had decided to play truant for the day, danced naughtily in the air. Okay, they said. Okay, said her dream man. Got your message. Here's mine. You can't miss it. High up in red letters for half of Orchard Road to see!

So he must have gone to borrow the waitress's brightest red lipstick. That moment of quick anger and jealousy should have been instead a moment of greatest pride in the beloved's quick thinking, in the show of creative energy ready to be mobilised, at a moment's notice, in the service of love. Henceforth, she would have deep regard for waitresses who had cherry-red lipsticks at the ready, to be of assistance to lovers. Henceforth, two letters of the English alphabet would claim special attention and tender regard.

He stood there in bright sunshine, his face beaming, his arms still swaying purposefully above his head, displaying the easeful grace of a victorious athlete acknowledging applause, continuing to flash the lipsticked assent, amid a babel of screeching brakes, tooting horns and angrily shaking fists.

Tears filled Li-ann's eyes. There could only be one explanation for the instantaneous, extraordinary response. His heart too must have been nurturing a dream; like hers, it knew when the moment came and it sprang to meet the other, in a conjoining arc of golden union.

29 February, 1980 – a Leap Year, when the word would forever take on the more exciting meaning of the lover's power to vault seemingly insuperable obstacles. As a child, she had been enthralled by the Chinese movies her mother had taken her to, showing legendary heroes and heroines flying through the air, leaping with the greatest ease over walls, temple roofs, mountain tops, and meeting, at last, in the radiant clouds of love's fulfilment.

A large cloud of smoke and grime from a bus hit her in the face and made her blink and cough. When she opened her eyes again, he was gone, seemingly swallowed up in the traffic that was flowing smoothly once more.

Four

Mrs Chang stood at the doorway of her daughter's room, not in the usual spying garb of pyjamas and hair-curlers, but beautifully coiffured, dressed and perfumed in readiness for a mahjong game with her friends. She would have been happy to forego the mahjong game to be part of what was apparently a prelude to some very exciting action. She stood watching Li-ann, in bra and panties, standing before the mirror and carefully applying mascara and lipstick, while nearby, on the bed, was laid out a very pretty pale blue dress with all its creases ironed out.

To the best of her memory, Mrs Chang had never witnessed such meticulous preparation for a date. Her face lit up with the sudden thought that her daughter had had a change of heart after all; one of the five big fish that she had so foolishly allowed to get away, must be the reason for this unwonted burst of enthusiastic self-adornment. Actually, there were only three left. Mrs Chang had learnt, much to her dismay, that the son of the High Court judge had already found a girlfriend, and that the son of the tycoon, T.C. Khor, was already engaged to be married. Still, there were the remaining three to provide hope. She made her inquiries in a voice quavering with high expectancy, and received a sharp "No!" from Li-ann to each uttered name.

"For goodness' sake, Mother," said Li-ann reproachfully.

"K.S.?" persisted Mrs Chang. She rated K.S. lowest because despite a good university degree in architecture, he chose to earn a meagre living giving scuba-diving lessons. Lately he had been visiting her daughter often and calling almost every day.

"If you could persuade him to take a regular job…" suggested Mrs Chang helpfully, and was rewarded with another explosion of exasperation: "Mother, I keep telling you it's none of them."

"Then who is it?"

"I don't know."

"You don't know the person you're going out on a date with?"

"That's right."

"Let's get it right. You're going out with a stranger? Just like that? Do you know his name?"

"No."

"Do you know his family?"

"No."

"Does he know you?"

"No."

Mrs Chang sat down weakly on her daughter's bed, overcome by an exasperation that was just one more in a long line of maternal grievances. She was slowly learning not to oppose her headstrong daughter, and to resort to other strategies, one being the use of biting sarcasm which proved more effective in eliciting the required information. So she said, "If it's that dream man in your head, bring him home, so I can pinch him and tell you if he's real."

Li-ann abandoned mascara to throw her arms around her mother's neck. "You'll never guess how I found him, and how he found me," she cried, her face radiant with joy. "But if you promise to behave, Mother, I'll tell you everything when I come back."

Mrs Chang gave a snort of disdain to hide a mounting curiosity and an even more dangerously mounting hope. There might be some decent man at the end of all the dream nonsense: who knows? She longed to give advice – be careful, don't give your address yet, he could be a conman, ask about his family, ask to see his identity card, etc., etc., – but prudently refrained. She watched her daughter go off in a glow of expectant hope and excitement.

Rushing through the doorway, Li-ann almost collided with K.S. coming in. He said he happened to be passing by and thought he would drop a magazine he had promised her. He looked at her and instantly guessed the reason for the glowing skin, the sparkling eyes. He gave a long deep whistle of admiration to hide the ache of a longing that was strangely all the greater for being mixed up with so much unfocused irritation.

"I hope he is short, ugly and speaks bad English," he said savagely. Li-ann had only time to pat his cheek and say, "Stop being so mean," before hurrying away.

She had actually rehearsed the presentation of herself several times in her head, to achieve the best first impression, said to be the most important because the most lasting. Every detail of dress and make-up had been carefully attuned to his taste which could be roughly extrapolated from his own style of dressing and the behaviour so far shown. Blue denim shirt, grey cotton pants bespoke a certain conservatism, which had resulted in her abandoning her first choice of a pink dress with puff sleeves for a light blue, slightly longer shirt-dress. The glasses, the neat haircut confirmed the general conservativeness; the title of the book which contained the two discernible words 'Philosophy' and 'Dialogues' told of much seriousness of thinking and taste, which suited her fine. (She recollected wincing a total of five times during a date with the tycoon's son who could not talk on any subject beyond his new car and the family holiday home in London.)

However, the unconventional creativity and brimming exuberance of that response of the wildly waving lipsticked palms in the midst of honking cars on a busy road, told of an intolerance for dullness in others, whether of appearance or behaviour. She was glad that she was anything but dull in either.

The long hours of careful preparation before the mirror, and of mental rehearsal, would be worth it.

She was ten minutes early. Vanity forbade giving the impression of over-eagerness, so she decided to wait by a pillar outside a shop on the road opposite, screened by darkness, yet having a good view of the appointed place of the meeting. Her watch showed five minutes to eight o'clock, then eight o'clock, ever so slowly. Into the minutes of tortuous waiting were crowded thoughts centred upon one chilling possibility: suppose he had decided not to come after all? Perhaps he was not sure that she had got his message after all, or had concluded that it was all one big joke which needed no pursuing further or he was being prevented from coming by a sudden attack of illness or an accident on the way…

At seven minutes past eight, she looked and caught her breath. There he was, rushing to take his place by the appointed table which, fortunately, was unoccupied. He stood and began looking around. She wondered what his mental image of her was like, that he was now trying to attach to a face among the faces around him. He looked worriedly at his watch several times. He was in a white shirt and khaki pants, and held a large black canvas bag in his hand, as if preparing to go on a trip.

According to the plan for the all-important presentation of herself, so carefully rehearsed, she would walk gracefully up to him, stand before him, smile and say, with just the right touch of sauciness, "You needn't have used so much of the waitress's lipstick." The reality was something less elegant. Crossing the road at an inopportune moment, she found herself standing petrified in front of a car that had screeched to an angry halt. She stood bewildered in a cacophony of screeches, before seeing someone rush up and drag her away. The young man dragged her to safety, to their appointed place by the table in the Blue Paradise Café, having braved chaotic traffic twice in a day, on her account.

"You may be adept at writing February 29 notes, but I see the skill does not extend to more practical things. Like watching for the traffic lights."

He knew! He had known her instantly, as she had known him. The heart has its reasons, it is said, which reason cannot understand. The heart also has a talent for spotting its mate in any confusion or maze, which reason cannot explain.

"Are you all right? Can I get you a drink?"

She stood staring at him, while her thoughts and feelings crackled inside her, like so many joyful fireworks.

"I'm Jeremy," he said.

"I'm Li-ann." She longed to ask him his Chinese name. Wu-er? No, that would have been asking too much of Fate which just now must be smiling at them.

She opened her mouth to say something, anything at all, to buy time to say something unconventional and unforgettable, and was immediately overwhelmed by what seemed like an urgent command.

"Two hours. I've got exactly two hours. Maybe a few more

minutes if I'm lucky," said Jeremy, looking at his watch and picking up the large black canvas bag from the floor of the café. His eyes were sparkling. She had never seen anyone who looked so well, so handsome, so happy. "Li-ann, now that we've found each other, will you be prepared to join me in a number of very important – I repeat, very important assignments, to be gloriously lost in the excitement of adventures in the night streets of Singapore? I don't promise safety, only fun and adventure."

'Found each other'. 'Gloriously lost.' No opening words upon a first meeting could resonate more with magic and romance. She found herself saying, "Okay."

"You met me a minute ago, and you agree to come with me, a total stranger, on a wild mission through Singapore, that has to be completed in two hours at most?"

"Yes."

"Well, what are we waiting for? I'm going to hail a cab right now. First stop, Cheng Koo Street, you know the slummy street in Chinatown famous for its fried *kuay teow* and sewer rats? You have exactly five seconds to change your mind and leave me. Five seconds up. Are you coming?"

"Yes."

His eloquence, in keeping with his brimming good spirits, was torrential, while her mounting excitement was expressed in meek monosyllables. How her heart was singing! A conventional getting-to-know-each-other over coffee at the assigned table in the assigned café would have been thrilling enough. Exchange of information regarding background, hobbies, interests, etc., etc., followed by an elaborate explanation from each side, of the unique circumstances of their meeting, followed, finally, by a warm, heart-to-heart how much meaning that commonplace expression now had for her! – talk about their dreams. But reality was even better than hope. It had all the elements of surprise and wonder and joyous expectation.

Her mother would have been appalled. She would have stopped the taxi, screamed for help, wrenched her free from a shocking escapade initiated by a total stranger, a madman.

"Cheng Koo Street," said Jeremy to the taximan. As the taxi speeded off he turned to Li-ann and held out his hand for a handshake. "We haven't had a proper introduction. My name is Jeremy Lee Yu-min."

"With a hyphen?"

"With a hyphen."

Five

The *kuay teow* seller whom Jeremy addressed familiarly as Uncle Bah Bah had a long towel draped around his neck, with which, at regular intervals in the frying of the *kuay teow*, in a giant pan over a roaring stove fire, he wiped his forehead and armpits.

The hot night air, the steam and smoke from a hundred other roaring stove fires, the hissing aromas of ready-to-be eaten crabs, prawns, oyster omelettes, suckling pig and duck noodles heaped high on huge plates rushed to the tables of hungrily expectant customers with their chopsticks and forks and spoons at the ready – all came together in a massive breakout of sweat and oil on the shimmering, portly body of Uncle Bah Bah, dad only in thin, cotton pyjama pants and a white cotton singlet rolled up to allow the freer breathing of a huge tub of a belly.

Uncle Bah Bah looking up from the frying, saw Jeremy and beamed.

"How's Kai Ma?" he boomed.

It was obvious that he knew Jeremy had come all the way to buy his *kuay teow* for this person. It was also obvious that Kai Ma was someone dear.

Li-ann, drinking in the sights and sounds and smells of this strangest of evenings in her life, allowing herself to be carried along on a warm rolling tide of delicious self-surrender to her dream-turned-substance, felt a substantial hand clasping hers, and felt no jealousy for Kai Ma. The name denoted safety. It meant 'godmother' and therefore elicited none of the sharp pangs that morning, caused, first by the young woman who had come to take a chair from his table, and then by the waitress who had lent him her lipstick. He had lavished his warmest, brightest smiles on each in turn. If he had smiled in the same way at the stray cat that had come in searching for dropped tidbits, or at the red plastic roses in a vase on each table, she would have been jealous of them too.

The heart, having staked out its territory, sniffed out rivals to destroy. But Kai Ma was, happily, no rival.

Jeremy seemed unable to stop talking about his godmother to Uncle Bah Bah. She listened, not as an intruder upon some private aspect of his life that she had had no part in, but as an interested, loving friend, soon to share that life. She listened, she stored up details, she tried to piece together a picture of the young man's background that he had so far resolutely closed to her while he took her on a wild swing through the night streets of Singapore. A western name, a hyphenated Chinese name, a godmother whom he loved enough to go to a great deal of trouble for. That was all he had divulged so far.

She listened attentively, and gathered more information. But it was the picture of the godmother, not of himself that built up. She was going to be ninety – the *kuay teow* seller said he would fry her the best *kuay teow* for her ninetieth birthday, with plenty of the cockles and lard bits that she liked so much. She lived in a home in Pagoda Lane, cared for by a woman who was totally devoted to her – the *kuay teow* seller claimed credit several times, for having been instrumental in getting her this devoted caregiver.

Li-ann had never understood the joy of anticipation so much as now; the best was yet to come. After the mad adventure, centred upon humouring an old woman – it really was not so much madness as loving kindness which made him even more attractive in her eyes – they would sit down by themselves at last and talk quietly, in whatever remaining time they had that evening. They would talk about themselves, get to know each other, make decisions, work out plans. For dreams, if they were not to vanish with sunlight, had to be quickly pinned down to earth, to take on the definite shape and contours of courtship and marriage.

Li-ann's mind worked feverishly but systematically, and scrolled out a neat programme of events. For love had to go calendrical some time; first meeting 29 February 1980, engagement 31 March 1980, wedding 28 February 1981. Li-ann decidedly favoured the last day of a month for both auspiciousness and delight.

The image of her mother suddenly appeared in her mind and made her smile. She already saw the massive confusion that the poor parent would be thrown into, being at once exhilarated by the prospect of a daughter's imminent marriage, and terrified by the mysteries surrounding the marriage partner. What! She could hear her mother screech. You're marrying someone and you don't know his family, what he does for a living, whether he can afford to support you, whether he owns a house or car. Find out. Do it carefully and discreetly. For instance, you could begin by asking…

The completion of her dream had little to do with these nonsensical little details which would not be allowed in their first getting-to-know-each-other talk. She would let her heart do all the talking, and listen for his heart to do all the responding. A glance, a touch, a word, a kiss – that might be all the confirmation she needed. Love's language needed no stringing out in long sentences, no tedious periphrases. "Hi, I'm Jeremy." "Hi, I'm Li-ann." The defining moment had been as simple as that.

Jeremy said, holding her with one hand and the packet of *kuay teow* in the other, "He's really persistent. A nuisance, but tonight, we oblige. It might be fun."

In her absorption with her thoughts, she had not noticed the itinerant fortune-teller who had attached himself to them like a leech, a scrawny old man with bad teeth and wearing a faded red silk robe with a dragon design and a skull cap with a phoenix design calculated to impress tourists enamoured of all things oriental. The man held up in his hands a canister of wooden fortune sticks. He invited Jeremy and Li-ann to shake out one stick each, and for five dollars, he would interpret the gods' messages to them. He looked closely at Jeremy's forehead, nose, ear-lobes, then held Li-ann's right palm in his hand and traced a forefinger delicately over it. He pronounced them both to have the luckiest features ever granted to mortals, and congratulated them in an effusion of surprise and goodwill, maintaining he had never met a couple so blessed in their lives.

Jeremy said, "The crook. Let's give him the five dollars and see what other promises he's going to make on behalf of the gods."

The man made them shake out a fortune stick each, and read the words inscribed on each stick with frowning, earnest stream of pure poetry from his mouth, as he stood in his silk robe and cap in the middle of the hot sounds and smells of Singapore's most famous open air, night food centre, magisterially waving a fan which he seemed to have produced from nowhere. Some tourists at a nearby table turned, watched and clapped their hands in delight.

"Let's go," said Jeremy, looking at his watch. "We're running short of time."

"Wait…" said the fortune-teller, and was sad to see them go before he could deliver the best gift of all from the gods, which he had been saving for the last. Not money, not longevity, not even the long line of male offspring, he was going to say in daring contradiction of a thousand-year-old tradition, but love. But they were gone.

"The crook," said Jeremy in the taxi, on their way to Pagoda Lane, and he threw back his head and laughed heartily. In the semi-darkness of the backseat in the taxi, he turned to look at Li-ann and give her hand a squeeze.

"I'm having so much fun, aren't you," he said, and moved closer to put his arm around her and press her head upon his shoulder. She lay contentedly against him as the taxi roared on. He was looking out of the window, at the shopfronts and night shoppers and trishawmen passing by, smiling all the time in an apparent state of supreme well-being, his fingers idly drumming on that part of her arm they had enclosed.

A thought struck her with force, and she beat it down instantly, as being most unwelcome. It had suddenly occurred to her that up till now, his entire demeanour towards her lacked the quality of a lover's. Even that act of gathering her into his arms in the semi-darkness of the taxi backseat lacked the ardour of a lover's embrace; he might have been hugging a child, a dear friend, a family member in need of solace.

And then the thought resurfaced as self-rebuke. Here was

she, fretting about not being kissed on a first date, when she had always resisted all romantic overtures on the first, the second, even the tenth date, as deplorable male presumption, always turning her face aside abruptly, peeling hands off knees and shoulders, wriggling her way out of overzealous arms.

This was different. She would not analyse the difference at this stage, only allow it to suffuse her entire body with a delicious sense of well-being. So she sighed and sank deeper into his arms and thought no more, while he continued to look out of the window, drum his fingers on her arm and whistle a happy tune.

"Here we are," he said, getting out of the taxi and helping her out. "33, Pagoda Lane. Watch Kai Ma's eyes light up at the sight of the kuay teow. And watch Ah Wan Cheh's eyes narrow in displeasure. She watches Kai Ma's diet like a hawk."

Jeremy Lee Yu-min, dragging her suddenly into his world and pulling her along with manic energy, never bothered to pause to explain. He disdainfully dispensed with the need for the proprieties and formalities of normal human transactions. Explanation was tedious to his blithe spirit.

He descended upon his Kai Ma with a whoop of affectionate joy. She was a frail, little old woman, with surprisingly smooth skin and tiny glittering black eyes that darted here and there, like some small, agitated animal. She recognised Jeremy at once, and began making shrill little sounds, stroking his cheeks affectionately. Ah Wan Cheh, who stood nearby watching, said she recognised nobody else, not even an adopted daughter who visited once a week. She remembered nothing else either. In the pitch darkness of her dementia, only one spot glowed brightly, and it glowed with a continuing love for the young man she had taken care of, from his birth. Kai Ma had been an old family servant elevated to the position of godmother in her old age.

This much Li-ann learnt from Jeremy himself as he undid the packet of *kuay teow* and invited the old woman to eat, drawing her attention to the special cockles and lard bits. Ah Wan Cheh said nervously, "It will most certainly give her diarrhoea," and Jeremy said, with a dismissive wave of his hand, "My Kai Ma gets to eat whatever she likes," and began helping her to spoon down the good stuff.

Li-ann watched. She was outside the moving little tableau of devotion earned and given, but she did not mind. An outsider, yet someone specially invited to share the cosy little intimacies of the scene. Jeremy turned to her and said, "I'm not sure I'll see her again. Canada's so far away. My mother has a story about how Kai Ma saved her life when she was a little girl. My father never believed it and thought it all pure superstition." And he turned back to helping thold woman with her food once more.

Reference to mother in the present tense, to father in the past tense. So there was a mother still living, and a father who had passed away. Canada – too far away to take a frail, old servant. Was he planning to emigrate to Canada?

The picture was building up, slowly, painstakingly. At the end of the evening's visit to Kai Ma, he would, in his usual, cheerfully disorganised manner, tell more, and the picture would be complete. The dream would have fully materialised. She would wait patiently, and enjoy the waiting.

Kai Ma stopped eating to stare at her, then got up, tottered towards her and reached up to hold her face in her hands. She felt the papery dryness of the old woman's hands, and looked into the bright little eyes.

"You must take good care of him," she quavered in a dialect that was familiar. "He is a very good boy who has never harmed anybody in his life. When he was three years old, a quarrelsome neighbour one day abused me and hit me on the head with a ladle. My Min Min saw the bruise on my head, ran to the neighbour's house, searched her out and kicked her in the buttocks. Then he ran back home to tell me what he had done."

Effortlessly, from the depths of a failed memory, the old woman pulled out one joyful tale after another of a little boy's devotion to his servant, radiant in its every remembered detail. She ended each tale with a plea, charged with urgency, as if there remained little time to caution the young: "You must take good care of my Min Min. As his wife you must honour and obey him. Young women today are not like the young women in my time. The gods have been specially kind to you, in giving you this good man."

It was a weird feeling – the realisation that in the course of an evening, two old persons with the wisdom of age, the fortune-teller in Cheng Koo Street and a ninety-year-old woman, had not only linked them together but singled them out as a favourite of the gods.

Ah Wan Cheh said, "She's tired, she must be put to bed now." But Kai Ma was not done yet. She continued to stand before Li-ann, and began to wag a severe little forefinger before her face. His rice to be steamed precisely thus, his fish porridge to be boiled to such and such a consistency, his trousers to be ironed in such a way that the pleats could cut, like knives. Her long litany of admonitions on wifely duties ended only when she had a fit of coughing, and then Ah Wan Cheh led her back to her room.

Jeremy bent down to whisper to Li-ann, "About the rice and the porridge and the knife pleats – she must have mistaken me for my grandfather or father. I would never be so demanding of a wife."

Here was a puzzle indeed, and a painful one, in the arduous task of building up the beloved's life story: was he already, or was he not yet married? The last words of Kai Ma before she was hustled off to bed, and the response they elicited, were most reassuring and settled that perturbing question once and for all.

"When you get married, you must not forget to tell your old Kai Ma."

"When I get married, my Kai Ma will be the first one to know."

Six

They were sitting at a small table drinking coffee in a café in the Singapore airport. Jeremy looked at his watch and said cheerfully, "Fifteen minutes. That's all the time we have. Then I fly off to Vancouver. My mother had not wanted me to come to Singapore, because there were so many pressing things to settle concerning the business. But I knew I had to see Kai Ma for the last time."

There it was again – the casual, disorganised scattering of information about himself, providing no context, no cohesion, to make any sense to the interested listener. She found herself becoming more an exasperated than an interested listener. She had been too patient and forbearing. Hang Vancouver. Hang the mother and the business. Hang Kai Ma.

Suddenly Li-ann felt a rising tide of annoyance. With fifteen minutes to go, he was taking too long to tell her he loved her, to tell her about that supreme moment of recognition, even before he met her, in the words of the note delivered to him, or in the image of her that must have scrolled across his mind when he flashed his OK sign in red in the air. Or the moment could have been in that first awareness of her actual bodily presence, as she stood bewildered in the midst of honking cars in the middle of a busy road and he rushed to rescue her. That supreme moment was being smothered out by a lot of irrelevancies.

Hers had come long before his, when, in a sudden burst of inspiration while listening to a long lecture, she had suddenly pulled him out of the clouds of imagination, lodged him firmly in her heart, and thereafter waited for the precise moment when dream would coincide with reality.

Fifteen minutes, he said, that's all the time we have. Fifteen minutes to celebrate love's breathtaking epiphany. In a very short while, all the preceding events concerning people and places and things she had had no interest in – Kai Ma and Uncle Bah Bah and *kuay teow* and Vancouver – like so many isolated pieces of a jigsaw puzzle floating about, would come together and group round the central, dominating piece, the story of their love. They were all but preludes to the final, grand climax, and were meaningful only in so far as they contributed to it.

Li-ann suppressed the rising annoyance and waited for that climax to come, as it must.

Jeremy said, "What a lovely day it has been," and reached to touch her hand. She said, trying to sound as casual as she could, "Tell me about this trip to Vancouver. You haven't breathed a word about it all evening. I was curious about the travelling bag."

Jeremy said dreamily, "You know, I've been so lucky. One of those guys who say a prayer, and it's heard immediately. There must be a nice Fate somewhere – probably a lady! – watching me. I was in this small town in Canada last year, waiting to catch a flight to Vancouver, and had four hours to kill. Four hours! And I had nowhere to go. I prayed, 'Dear God' – or perhaps I said, 'Dear Lady Fate, send me something, someone, to kill this boredom.' And hey presto! A woman appeared with a dog that took a liking to me. We played. I taught it tricks. I've never seen a more intelligent creature. By the time I was ready to leave, we had become such buddies that I would have taken it home if the woman had let me. And today, in the Blue Paradise Café, I said to myself, 'This is my last and dullest day in Singapore. I wish something would happen.' And hey presto again! A small, skinny Indian boy came up with your note, which is the most tantalising I've ever seen. I could not have asked for anything better. I thought, 'Here is someone I just have to meet, by hook or by crook,' and instantly, the idea of the lipstick came to me."

The annoyance returned and rose dangerously, a bitter upwelling stream that was the bitterer for its being entirely unnoticed Jeremy continued, with no abatement of the exuberant enjoyment of his good luck, "It could have been such a boring day! Singapore sometimes bores me to tears. And then your funny little note appeared. And, even better, you appeared. Only two hours left! But I was determined to make the best use of them with you. You have been such a fun companion."

There were the beginnings of angry, hot tears in her eyes, of an angry sharpening of her tongue ready to lash out in all its fury. So she had been no more than a diversion, a pleasant plaything for warding off boredom. He had wanted amusement, like an over-indulged child, and his tutelary spirit, some force as frivolous-minded as himself, had humoured him. That was all that their encounter had amounted to. A distraction. An interim thing, not even worthy of being called an interlude, which would be forgotten as soon as it had served its purpose. He was nothing more than a spoilt, selfish, self-centred young man who was used to having all his whims and fancies pandered to. He had trifled with her in the most callous manner.

Jeremy, still oblivious of her darkening mood, once more

spoke laughingly about the friendly, intelligent dog he had befriended. "Its name was Spookie – now isn't that a weird name?" He was then distracted by something that looked like a stain on his sleeve and spent the next minute trying to get it off.

She could have stood up there and then, shouted something at him and left the table. But she found herself in a paralysis of confusion and pain that left her still maintaining her quiet position in the chair, still listening to this impossible man's impossible chatter. It was preposterous, her being put in the same category as a friendly dog – in effect he was doing precisely that – but still she said nothing, while the tears gathered and the throat tightened unbearably.

Now he noticed. "Hey, you're crying! What's the matter? Have I said something wrong? Please forgive me." He was at her side in a moment, having got up with such abruptness that his chair had fallen over. The mood of exhilaration had vanished. He was all solicitous concern. He tried to take her into his arms to stop the tears, and she pushed him away. Now the tears were flowing freely. She began to sob uncontrollably.

"Please, please, Li-ann, don't cry," cried Jeremy in great alarm. "Talk to me. Tell me what's upset you."

You! You! She wanted to scream. Everything about you is upsetting me.

"I'm sorry," said Jeremy. No longer his usual laughing, exuberant self he was almost unrecognisable in the intensity of his shock which gave his face a strange pallor and made him look older. He stood helplessly looking at her, watching for any sign of relenting that would allow him to put his arms around her, which clearly he very much wanted to do. "I'm sorry for being such a selfish beast. Subjecting you to all the madness of the rush. Dragging you along for my own selfish enjoyment. It was extremely presumptuous of me. Will you forgive me?"

Contrition is cheap and could buy forgiveness cheaply. It would have been easier for her to snap, "Stop this hypocrisy," and walk away that instant.

But the man standing before her had not an iota of guile in his body. Anybody could see that. He was as artless as a child.

Contrition was both irrelevant and useless to her. If suddenly, as if awakening to some long dormant impulse, he had said, "I love you," the situation would have been saved. She continued to cry softly, overwhelmed by a confusion of feelings all the more painful for their being despised in others as a sign of weakness.

"Will you allow me to write to you from Vancouver?"

He had exhausted present methods of appeasement and was ready to try whatever others he could think of. He was ready to go the whole way of expiation, even if still unclear about what he was expiating for. In the angry rejection of his efforts to touch her, one part of her reached out towards this generosity of spirit that would ever make him likeable in the general carelessness of his self-indulgent life.

"I would invite you to my wedding, if you would come. Would you?"

Now he was being both desperate and ludicrous. His need to be forgiven was making him come up with laughable unrealistic conciliations. Attend his wedding, he said, and thought he was offering a palliative to her pain. She would hate the word ever afterwards and associate it with the final, bitter retreat of a dream.

"Kai Ma mistook you for Florence," he said with a little laugh, in a foolish attempt to try humour where all else had failed. "That was why she went on and on about the duties of a good wife. You remember that bit about the fish porridge?"

His naivete was astonishing. He actually thought he was succeeding with the humour and threw in another episode related to Kai Ma and Florence. He went into lengthy explanation which she would have stopped her ears against. Stop! she wanted to scream. Stop! Don't you know how it hurts me to hear all this?

He went on talking, this golden boy whose golden life was all planned and laid out beautifully for him by others, so that, like the over-protected prince in the fairy tale, he had no idea of the thorns and cuts and bruises in the real world.

Florence was his fiancée. She was the daughter of his parents' very close friends who had emigrated to Vancouver more than ten years ago. After his father's death, his mother decided to leave Singapore and join them, actually buying a house next door to theirs. That was the degree of the closeness. And then – he wasn't sure whether it was his mother who first put the idea in his head – the possibility of the two families being united through a union of their children, came up and rapidly shaped into a distinct probability. He and Florence who had in fact been in kindergarten together began to see each other more often. They would be married very soon, almost as soon as he returned to Vancouver. His mother who had survived a major operation said she had never felt so well or been so happy in her life. She kept saying she wished his father were alive to share the happiness. She and Florence had not wanted him to come to Singapore to see Kai Ma, but he had insisted, believing it would be his last time.

The young man who had throughout the evening dispensed with all explanation in a bravado of unconventionality, was now meekly offering her an abundance of it. When he finished, he stood silently watching her, the urgent need to be forgiven, like an anxious child's, written all over his face.

By now his world and hers had moved so far apart from each other that she doubted any explanation on her part or his, would serve any purpose. They would always be separated by a chasm. of misunderstanding, and shout explanations uselessly across a frightening void.

Suddenly she felt very tired. It was the exhaustion of presiding over a dream's demise. Her dream had shattered massively against reality, and now lay in a hundred shards around her. She was too tired to pick up the pieces. All she wanted was to go home, crawl into bed and go to sleep. It would be the sleep of exhaustion, but would allow some reprieve from the pain that was threatening to engulf her. She would have to deal with it at some time. But for now, she wanted to close her eyes, empty her mind and calm her heart in sleep.

"Li-Ann, please talk to me. Please say something," said Jeremy and he began to look nervously at his watch. The announcement came, as expected: "Will all passengers boarding Flight..."

She got up from the table, pale and shaken. "I loved you so much," she found herself saying. "So much and so foolishly." She looked around forlornly and said, "I'll always remember 29 February 1980 as the saddest day in my life." The day had begun so brightly that its ending bleakness was just too much to bear. It must have been the pain that was expressing itself in this sad confession, so alien to her proud nature. She could hear her own voice, coming from a distance, detached from her body. "I loved you...", "I'll always remember..." A dream consigned to the past, a future made up of hopeless remembrance, when only the present should be love's language and its celebration. Her voice, coming from a distance, made her pause to catch its mournful tones.

The surreality of it all had a strange tranquillising effect on her; she was calmly watching and listening to herself calmly observing a woman struggling with two large suitcases and trying to keep pace with a rapidly walking man. Then she picked up her handbag from the table and got ready to leave. Saying goodbye to a dream that has died could be effected by a small, slow action. Just pick up your handbag and leave.

She turned and walked away, breaking into a run only when from the corner of her eye she saw him hurrying towards her. She caught a glimpse of his pale, distraught face, and would believe him if he said, "I'm in pain too, for causing so much of it."

If only! If he could give her cause to believe that the pain was born of love, not guilt, the situation, even at this moment, could be saved.

She turned briefly, in response to a shout. For he was shouting now in a sudden access of recklessness mixed with hope. "Wait, Li-ann, please wait. I have something to tell you."

She continued to hurry away, almost knocking down a child, dressed warmly for a long distance flight, clutching an old teddy bear. "Li-ann, I've got an idea! Please hear it." He was yelling now, across a vast expanse of space filled with hurrying passengers who only briefly turned to see what the commotion was about.

An idea, he said. An idea was something that came from the head. All she wanted to hear, in these last desperate moments, was something from the heart.

"I promise you that I will come to Singapore every 29 February, to see you. Same table, same café, same time." For the second time that day, people turned and stared at him. The amplified voice making routine announcements took on an appropriate urgency: "Last call for Flight…", and Li-ann saw him waving to her before rushing away. There was no love behind that mad promise, only wrenching remorse. She had no need for remorse.

Promises, promises. And what of the supposedly benign Fate who had filled her with hope and led her to him that morning, only to flee in fright, like a prankster panicking when he sees his prank suddenly going all wrong?

Promises, promises. She would teach her heart to be more wary.

Seven

On Christmas Eve, 1983, Li-ann attended a party given by Kim who had remained her closest friend despite dropping out of the university to marry one Danny Sim Fook Kuan and going to live abroad for a year.

It was what was generally called a whirlwind courtship and marriage. Danny came roaring in his red sports car to pick her up for dinner after an introduction the day before, came roaring after that every day for a full month in a variety of sleek, shiny cars, bearing expensive gifts of flowers and perfume, and proposed marriage on the last day of the month. He married her, two months later, at a glittering wedding banquet irt the hotel owned by his father, and whisked her off on a honeymoon in Europe from which they returned, a year later, to settle down in Singapore.

Through it all, Kim who had been the undisputed, domineering leader of The Group, as Li-ann and her former university mates called themselves, remained dazed and wide eyed, gratefully submitting to a bombardment of wealth, prestige and influence never dreamt of before. She said, "Yes, Danny," or "Yes, my darling," in an impossibly sweet voice. Danny told The Group it had been Kim's dimples that had first attracted him, setting off a flurry of private debates among the girls as to what ultimately attracted men to women. It was Jennie whose tongue could be both sharp and unkind, who had remarked that a playboy, fatigued by a surfeit of beautiful women, was ready to settle down with a plain woman of solid character who happened to have pretty dimples.

In any case, Kim was supremely happy, the epitome of female success in Singapore. Ensconced in a huge house with a sprawling garden that her parents, living in their government subsidised two-room flat would never have dreamt of, she invited her friends for lunches and dinners, which always culminated in a trip upstairs to view her enormous bedroom with its enormous wardrobe of fine dresses and shoes and handbags. On Christmas Eve 1983, there was an additional item for viewing – a baby's room with crib, furniture and toys in readiness. For Kim was proudly pregnant, and the dinner was as much to celebrate the pregnancy as the festive season.

So much proof of the largesse of marriage ought to be working its effects on the minds and hearts of those still single. Male munificence and loving fidelity formed that rarest of combinations often referred to as luck. But the truth was that Danny Sim Fook Kuan, only a year and a half after marriage, was off again on his riotous rounds of dating glamorous women, especially models in Hong Kong, away from the prying eyes and gossiping tongues in Singapore. Kim did not know, or preferred not to know.

It would only be in the 90s, after three children and much anguished thinking that she considered divorce. She had to grit her teeth through the greatest humiliation of her life, when her husband cheerfully admitted to his numerous affairs, told her she was no longer sexually attractive to him, and offered to settle a very large sum on her and the children. Clean him out, clean the bastard out, said her family. By the time it was all over, she had lost fifteen pounds and looked ten years older. She whimpered, when her friends comforted her, "I wish with all my heart I had never dropped out of university." But that would be in 1994; in December 1983, Kim pronounced herself the luckiest and happiest woman in Singapore.

The happiness, shining in her eyes, skin and hair, was a sharp contrast to Li-ann's dull-eyed passivity. Everybody wanted to be nice to Li-ann, since everybody knew but did not dare to ask about the sad little affair related to her dream man, which, even after almost four years, the poor girl seemed unable to get over. They remembered having ruthlessly teased her about it; now none of them would have the heart to say, "We told you so about all that dream man nonsense."

Kim tried to distract her with talk, chatting interminably about her fast-living in-laws, swinging wildly between exuberant boasting about their fabulous shopping sprees in London, Paris and Hong Kong, and grave admission of the truth of those dreadful rumours about a mentally retarded son who had raped the family maid.

Suneetha, who was having a very satisfying relationship with a Norwegian engineer working in an oil company, in secret defiance of strict, conservative parents, patted her reassuringly on the shoulder several times.

Jennie, who in 1980 had sworn to dish out to her man the exact amount of love he had given her and who was now exceeding her target by generous margins, simply pretended to know nothing about Li-ann's heartbreaking experience, and asked her whether she intended to take up the university's offer of a scholarship for post-graduate studies in an affiliated university in Britain. The prestigious offer had directly followed her graduating with a First Class Honours.

"I don't know," said Li-ann.

"I would if I were you," said Jennie, and then committed the supreme indelicacy of adding, "Two years away from Singapore. Might be just what you need."

"I don't know," said Li-ann again.

Kim, sensing that the conversation had taken a wrong turn, set it right again by announcing, with a light tapping of her stomach, "Li-ann, you'll be the first Godma to my first baby. For my next, it will be you, Suneetha. And then you, Jennie." In support of Singapore's new population policy which was a total reversal of the old one of limiting women to only two children, Kim was freely dispensing godmotherships for at least three. She laughed heartily, and thereafter the conversation steered clear of unhappy topics, as they all moved upstairs to view the baby's room.

"Girls," said Li-ann. "Look at me." They all turned in surprise from the lace-covered bassinet over which they had been cooing to look at her.

"Girls," said Li-ann. "I know you're dying to ask me. Ask. Let's have the first question." They looked at each other quizzically, and then faced her again, their expressions in a careful state of suspension, to be rearranged as smiles or frowns of sympathetic concern, depending on what she was going to say next.

"Okay, Jennie," said Li-ann, sounding more animated than usual, so that they exchanged sly questioning glances with one another again. "You're the first. Ask."

Jennie said, "Is it about that Dream Man of yours?"

"Dream Man's no more. Out of my system. No kidding. Now aren't you glad to hear that, girls? I'm okay now." They crowded around her and gave her hugs, to indicate their relief and joy.

"Okay, Kim. Now tell me about that millionaire friend of your husband whom you've been dying to matchmake with me. His income? Number of cars? My mother will bless you for the rest of her life." They laughed and hugged again, in a renewal of camaraderie. The errant member of The Group had been reinstated.

On the morning of the first day of 1984, Li-ann sleepily woke up to a call from K.S. "Happy New Year!" he said brightly "Now listen very carefully. You'd told me twice before that you wanted to spend the day quietly. But since you've stood my stubbornness for so long, I might as well go on with it. So how about a lunch today at the Belvedere? Or tea? Dinner? Brunch? A meal with no name, as long as it is for two people?" K.S. had kept his wry sense of humour all these years.

"No thanks, K.S. I'm rather tired. I'm just going to relax with a book."

"One more dose of the stubbornness coming up! Please, Li-ann. They have the best crayfish at the Belvedere. And don't deny that crayfish is your favourite."

"No thanks, K.S."

"Now it's going to be bluntness added to the stubbornness. Of a brutal sort too. Tell me, Li-ann, how long are you going to mourn for that good-for-nothing dream man?"

She could have said, "None of your business!" and hung up in annoyance. But there was something about K.S. that made annoyance irrelevant. It was his devastating honesty which made him the most likeable person she had ever met. It made him say exactly what he felt, totally independently of what others might feel, so that, along the way, he offended many people.

Li-ann much preferred his brusque frankness about her

problem to the delicate tiptoeing around it by her friends. Or perhaps it was because the frankness had a desperate quality, which touched her heart: he had remained steadfast in his devotion to her, through her obsession with another man over these many years. K.S. was one of those men who loved not wisely, but too well.

She owed it to him to reciprocate with her own brand of frankness, softened by a genuine liking for this good, loyal man who would do anything to win her love: "Dear, dear K.S. Why don't you just give up on me? I'm a hopeless case!"

It was the tenacity of a lover's hope that made him say to himself, "As long as she allows me to see her, there's still a chance," and the sly desire to exploit female vanity that made him say aloud, " Give up on you? You might as well ask me to give up breathing." The greater the vanity, the more effective the hyperbole.

Patience, thought K.S., with new determination. That was chiefly it. You could always wear down a woman's resistance with patience. A woman, by virtue of her biology as procreative and nurturative being, was born with an immense capacity for caring and could be made to feel guilty if she did not love a good man back. A woman's sense of guilt worked in a man's favour.

K.S. had got it all worked out. But the real reason for the patient wait, he thought with a sigh, was simply that he loved her so much. She was worth all the waiting in the world. She was an impossible dreamer absurdly pining for a man she had met and lost within twenty four hours. But he could not think of any woman he wanted so much to marry and cherish for the rest of his life. K.S. thought, with another sigh, that his love too had its own absurdity.

Her mother was clearly more prepared for direct talk than he was. Pulling him aside one evening as he was waiting for Li-ann to come out of her room, she said, "So?" He knew what she meant. Unable to get anything out of her daughter about the actual status of their relationship, she was resorting to a direct confrontation of him.

"No," he said. He went on to say that they were only friends. At least that was what Li-ann wanted.

Mrs Chang frowned a little and after some hesitation said, "You must not get offended with me, K.S., if I say this to you. You visit my Li-ann so often that people will think you are both going steady so…"

She paused, not quite sure how to go on, and K.S. completed the admonition for her, "So men will not come courting Li-ann? Don't worry, Mrs Chang. Your daughter and I are just friends. She doesn't want to marry me." He decided that much as he loved the daughter, he was evincing a genuine dislike for the mother.

Mrs Chang took the opportunity to give advice on something she had been meaning to talk to him about for a long time, "K.S., you must not get offended with me if I say that with your good university degree, you should not be just a scuba-diving instructor…"

"It's even worse, Mrs Chang. I'm no longer that. I'm unemployed."

Mrs Chang fled in despair and disgust. The irresponsibility of young people was unbelievable. Knowing only a little about the dismal event of 1980, helplessly watching her daughter go through a period of mourning and loss – how needless, how foolish, over a total stranger, over a ridiculous schoolgirl fantasy! – Mrs Chang had watched the years go by – 1981, 1982, 1983 – with increasing concern, for none yielded a boyfriend or even the possibility of one. Li-ann had kept to herself and occasionally agreed to go out with only K.S. who was now more tiresome fixture than bright promise. What on earth did her daughter who was approaching twenty six, intend to do with her life?

"We mothers are the first to feel, and the last to know," she whined to her mahjong friends. She bent her head, to show a distinct grey patch in her dark, neatly permed hair. "All this from worrying about Li-ann."

One of the friends tried to offer comfort which could only add to the vexation. "That friend of hers, Kim, isn't half as beautiful as your Li-ann." Mothers would, for years, look at Kim's mother with a sideways glance of envy, and resent her preening herself with the wealth that flowed from her prosperously married daughter, but would only remember, years later when the scandal broke and the break-up was reported in the newspapers, that they had always cautioned their daughters against marrying rich, useless playboys.

K.S. said to Li-ann, "Listen to my proposition. There are beginning to be too many singles around in Singapore shunning marriage. Why don't you marry me, so that together we can restore faith in that institution?" and had a pillow pushed into his face, as in the old days.

In the old days, he could joke about the dream man whom she had so exuberantly and frankly told him about, with all the innocence of an ardent schoolgirl. Now uneasiness on both sides precluded any mention. Still, annoyance with the troublesome and departed dream lover sometimes got the better of K.S. and he was ready to unleash his choicest sarcasms. He wished heartily she had never told him about this obnoxious character who had trifled with a young girl's emotions and left such a mess behind. Yet the victim did not find the perpetrator at all obnoxious. Indeed, so insidiously had he insinuated himself into her thoughts and feelings that she actually continued to hold him in some kind of awed fascination. That was the really exasperating part.

She kept talking about the strange promise he had shouted out at the airport. Every 29 February. Same table, same café, same time. She had never told anybody else about it. "What do you think? What can you make of it?"

He could see she had been thinking a great deal about it. "A lot of nonsense. The product of an over-active imagination, not to mention an over-developed ego."

At the beginning of February, she again spoke to him about it. She had become obsessed with the insane promise. The man, whom he had never seen and wished never to see, was becoming hateful. K.S. said impatiently, "I don't want to hear anything about this man. As far as I'm concerned, he doesn't exist. Or only as a thorn in my side, that I can't seem able to pull out."

But even K.S.'s devotion had its limits. He lapsed into a sullen silence, and then got up to leave.

Li-ann said, "I'm sorry, K.S. I really am."

He said, almost with a snarl, "If I get my arithmetic right, this is the hundred and tenth sorry in a very long series," adding bitterly, "you might as well dispense with them, for all the sincerity you feel."

"Wait," said Li-ann as K.S. was at the door. "Wait."

He turned to look sulkily at her. There was a trembling defiance in her voice as she said, "What about a dinner date on 29 February, in the Blue Paradise Café."

K.S. said, "I haven't the slightest idea what you're up to, Li-ann, but you're not going to use me," and slammed the door behind him.

Eight

The heart which had for so long been her guide in her decisions, had relinquished that role to the head, that organ for cool, detached deliberation, which should indeed have been trusted in the first place, to avoid all the pain of a lost dream.

So it was with the head that Li-ann, with the approach of 29 February 1984, arrived at her decision to go to the Blue Paradise Café. The reasoning had gone like this. If she did not go, she would never know whether Jeremy had kept his promise. The torment of never knowing would be the greatest torment of all, a horrible question mark spawning other question marks that would hang over all her thought and ruin her peace of mind forever. If she did go she would risk a second heartbreak even before the first had healed. For she might not find him there after all. A crazy promise had been just that, forgotten as soon as he had got on the plane and headed for another country and another life. Even if he kept the promise, came and met up with her again in the Blue Paradise Café, he might spend all his time there talking about his wife Florence and how happy he was, all the while unaware, in his usual cheerful thoughtlessness, of the humiliation of her position as a still single, still hopeful female who was having her hopes dashed in her face a second time.

Supposing I go. Supposing I don't. Supposing I go but hide somewhere just to satisfy my curiosity. Supposing he comes and I go to meet him, but I snub him outright. Her mind went through each of the options and dismissed them, one by one, as unworkable.

And then, as she was half-listening to K.S. who was sitting next to her on the sofa, an idea had suddenly occurred to her as one more option, better than all the rest. A dinner date with K.S. Same table, same café, same time. Let Jeremy Lee Yu-min who had left her so suddenly and callously on 29 February 1980, return that same date in 1984, to find her with another man. The presence of K.S. would redress the inequality in their positions: you with Florence, me with K.S. She might even hint that she was already married or about to be married to K.S. She would smile at him, and relish thereafter the memory of the look of shock and angry jealousy. For it was part of a man's territoriality to want both a wife and a line-up of women hopelessly swooning over him. She would play the same game. It would be a triumph that would go some way towards the healing of a wound that seemed unhealable after four years. She needed his pain to cancel out hers.

The head had thought of a strategy of savage revenge on behalf of the heart.

The idea was brilliant! She nursed it for a day or two, waiting for K.S. to visit. But as soon as she uttered it aloud to him, as they sat together on their favourite sofa, and saw his startled, angry reaction, she saw it in all its inanity and insensitivity, and felt ashamed of herself How could she even think of doing such a thing to K.S.? "Wait," she had cried out, but he had left fuming.

That evening she had called to apologise, but it was his mother who picked up the phone. She said that K.S. had gone away somewhere on a scuba-diving instruction course and would not be back for days, or weeks. Her voice had the guardedness of one giving information based on precise, strict instructions. "Where?" Li-ann asked, determined to pursue him, wherever he was, with her apology. His honest love for her made her scheme of exploitation that much more deplorable. She actually felt sick with remorse.

It was frightening – this mix of powerful emotions revolving around the two men in her life, one absent and yearned for, the other present and yearning. The maelstrom took her on wild, criss-crossing trajectories of anger, pain, sadness, longing, hope, fear, pity and guilt, that left her totally exhausted.

The heart was insuppressible, for sure. In the dreams at night, it once more asserted itself forcefully, reclaiming the happiness it had known. Tender memories suppressed during the waking hours of her busy life as a teacher in the National Junior College, came crowding back at night, like a flock of noisy birds newly released from their cage.

Her dreams had an editing power, selecting out the pain, keeping in only the pleasure. Thus she relived only the earlier part of the evening of 29 February 1980, before the joy had got clouded. The dreams had a focusing power too, highlighting the best and tenderest moment. She saw herself in Jeremy's arms at the back of the taxi, wriggling deeper and deeper into the pure warmth and comfort of his embrace. It was a sensation so palpably real that when she woke up, it continued to course, like a warm stream, through her entire body.

Dreams are not supposed to carry smells. But the pungency of the *kuay teow* sizzling in garlic oil in Uncle Bah Bah's frying pan, lingered long in her nostrils, chiefly because it coincided with that delicious moment when Jeremy, up till then holding her hand, suddenly brought it up to his cheek for a playful rub against the first signs of unshavenness. In real time, there had been a quick, laughing withdrawal by soft skin from prickliness; in dream time, the contact enlarged from mere playful touch of hand and cheek into something distinctly sensual. She saw herself and him together on a sofa and felt not only his arms around her, but a thigh flung across hers, lips pressed against hers.

Waking, she thought, "Dreams are useless," and tried to dislodge them from memory. Work, work. That was it. She needed work to distract her. Throwing herself fully into the many activities of teaching and interacting with her students in the junior college, marking their written assignments, preparing them for examinations, joining them in the extra-curricular activities of netball and debating and drama should provide the cure.

"Take this; it's very good," said her mother brightly, coming in with a steaming bowl of something. Nowadays Mrs Chang never asked questions, never gave advice, but only offered nutritious chicken soup and cooling herbal drinks to salve a broken heart. Nowadays Li-ann never protested nor raised her voice in exasperated response. She threw her arms around her mother's neck, almost upsetting the chicken soup, and said with something between a laugh and a sob, " Mothers are a girl's best friend," but stopped short of opening her heart.

"Go on," said her head, and it meant, "Go on with your plan of revisiting all those places – Blue Paradise Café, Cheng Koo Street, Pagoda Lane. Don't leave out any."

She remembered a story she had read as a child, about a little boy who was frightened of an old, gnarled tree in a neighbour's yard, and who overcame his fear by simply doing ten friendly things with the tree, including putting his arms around its ugly, knotted trunk and swinging from one of its branches.

It was not fear of the places that she wanted to overcome, but the sadness their memories evoked. She had no need to do friendly things with them, only to say to them, "There! I've made myself come here again. Now I can walk away."

"Where are you going?" said her mother, watching her pick up her car keys and getting ready to go out.

"Oh, nowhere in particular," she replied.

The Blue Paradise Café was still there, unchanged after four years, except for a new coat of paint which was a bright pink, and new tables and chairs in white plastic. She looked at the spot where his table used to be and wondered, if he came back, whether he would remember it. She looked at the waitresses, and saw that the lender of the bright red lipstick was no longer there. Or perhaps she was, but unrecognisable after four years of slaving at a mean little job. The uniform was still pink gingham.

Cheng Koo Street was in the process of being cleaned up and given a thorough overhaul in some major programme of urban renewal by the government. While waiting to be relocated, the food sellers were clearly doing their best to ensure that loyal customers who had been coming for ten, fifteen, twenty years for their favourite duck noodles or chicken rice or turtle soup would manage to sniff out their stalls, wherever the relocation. Li-ann looked for Uncle Bah Bah's *kuay teow* stall, and saw it was still there, but attended by a younger man, probably the son. Had Uncle Bah Bah passed away?

Driving along in her car, she was about to turn into Pagoda Lane when she suddenly swerved and did a U-turn. She had decided that she never wanted to see the place again. It would be too depressing. In any case, Kai Ma was probably long dead and gone.

But the old woman who had mistaken her for Florence and advised her to be a good wife to Jeremy was apparently determined to be noticed. As soon as Li-ann reached home and settled down to read The Straits Times, she saw Kai Ma's picture. Ordinarily, she did not look at the obituaries page. Today, she did and saw the photograph of a grave-looking old woman, indistinguishable from hundreds of others in their neat dark samfoo blouses, with hair severely combed back into a bun at the back, eyebrows neatly plucked into two thin moon arches, and tiny jade studs on the ear-lobes. Kai Ma had died just the week before, at the ripe age of ninety four. The obituary for an old family servant who had apparently died single and childless, made mention of a long line of adopted sons and daughters to mourn the loss. His name jumped up at her and sent a little *frisson* through her entire being: Jeremy Matthew Lee Yu-min. Now the 'Matthew' was an additional bit of information after all these years.

Had he come to Singapore for the funeral? If so, had he thought of her? If he had thought of her and wanted to see her again, would he have once again used that sparkling creative mind and energy to track her down?

The questions, coming one after the other, could not be stemmed in their flow. They quickly enlarged into a speculative picture of his life in Vancouver. So there were the pampering mother and in-laws, the wife, the business, the constant travelling, the self-indulgence, the insuppressible high spirits, the rare gift of attracting people and making them like him. She wondered if he was in love with his wife. Probably not. Florence seemed to have been his mother's choice. But that would in no way diminish this happy man's large appetite and enjoyment of life. He remained happy by simply allowing Fate to carry him along, and Fate had never failed him. If there were one mortal on earth who was spared the pain of thwarted plans, it was Jeremy Matthew Lee Yu-min.

Did he have children? How many? Was he happy, truly happy? She would dearly love to know.

What would be the nature of their second meeting, in circumstances so different from the first? Would he, a married man, still take her on a jaunty trip through town, or come up with some other surprise? If he decided only to talk, what would they talk about?

On the evening of 29 February 1984, as she took her place at the designated table in the Blue Paradise Café, Li-ann's heart was pounding so violently that she thought everyone around could hear. She had never been so nervous in her life. Her watch showed fifteen minutes past eight. Her plan had gone all wrong. She had only intended to wait behind a pillar, as she had done four years back, to watch for his arrival. After ten minutes, the anxiety had become so unbearable that she had to do something. She found herself, gasping and perspiring, making straight for the café and sitting down at the table in the remembered spot. She had no idea about what to do beyond the urgent need to claim the table quickly, before others could do so.

She ordered a coffee and drank it in little sips, in between looking at her watch and doing a quick survey of the place with her eyes, without so much as a slight movement of her head. The minutes ticked by ever so slowly. Twenty past eight. Half past eight. A quarter to nine. So he was not coming after all. So the promise was no promise after all.

The decision about whether to go or stay a little while longer was itself a tedious slow-moving process, making her appear, even to the most casual observer in the café, a pathetic bundle of nerves. She felt a warm flush spreading over her cheeks and neck, and hot tears pricking her eyes.

"May I –" She jumped up with such violence that she knocked over the vase of plastic flowers on the table. Disappointment often makes its sufferer lash out in fury. But the disappointment on seeing K.S. was mixed with so much relief that Li-ann actually found herself crying out, "Oh, K.S., I'm so glad to see you!"

He said, "I'm sorry I behaved so badly," meaning both the storming out in anger and the lie he had made his mother tell her on the phone. "I was all the time in Singapore. I missed you badly," he said simply, and then noticed the tears in her eyes. He reached out to press her hands. "Why, they're cold," he said and warmed them with his.

It would never occur to K.S., in the generosity of his love for her, to say, "Hadn't I warned you?" He would, at a more appropriate time, unleash the full range of the savage epithets reserved for one who, by causing pain for years to a girl he loved, had become his enemy. Unable to blame the girl for her part in the pain, he concentrated his wrath on the enemy. But now he would show restraint. Now, only words of the gentlest, most tactful kind, were called for. Or rather, no words, but a tender understanding silence. He had learnt that that worked better with her. So he continued to hold her hands and massaged them expertly, to restore their warmth.

"K.S., I'm sorry," said Li-ann, and added, with a little laugh, amidst the tears, "my hundred and twentieth, I think." It would not do for either of them ever again to refer to the ghastly stratagem of vengeance that had backfired so miserably.

"Would you like to eat? Shall I order something?" said K.S.

"No, I'm not hungry. What about you?" said Li-ann.

Their efforts to tiptoe around the embarrassment and induce the normality of a regular dinner date could not be sustained, at least on her part. Her eyes began now to brim with tears, her lips trembled and she blurted out, in the discharge of an overburdened heart, "Oh, K.S., I've been such a fool. I'm so unhappy!"

He moved his chair closer to hers, to whisper reassuringly in her ear, "It's okay, it's okay." Still holding her hands tightly, he did not know what else to say, so he repeated, "Everything's going to be okay." Her admission, so spontaneously made, pleased him. Admission was the first necessary step in the gigantic task of dismantling that superstructure of false hopes so foolishly built and maintained over the years.

By now there were people turning round to look at them, a few smiling benignly in the belief that they had just witnessed a happy conclusion to a lovers' quarrel. Li-ann who was no longer crying said, "K.S., you're so good to me," and he replied, with a great show of nonchalance, "Think nothing of it, dear girl!" and patted her on the arm.

He had never felt happier. He liked very much the sensation of her hands trustingly curled up in his, her head tilted towards his shoulder, almost touching it. The pain of finding her in her futile wait alone in the café had vanished.

Against his strongest instincts of self-pride and self preservation, he was worshipping a girl who was a declared worshipper of another. But the situation, at last, was changing. Let the failed rendezvous with that Canadian – he could not bring himself to utter the enemy's name – deal the final death blow to her folly. He was glad that against his strongest instincts, he had decided to go to the Blue Paradise Café that evening, after all. It had been a wrenching decision that had to struggle against the self taunt screaming in his ears: "She's making use of you to get another, and you go along, like a sheep to the slaughter?" Now all that suffering would be worth it. Together, they would demolish a dream that had for too long stood between them, and send it crashing to its deserved fate.

He said, looking into her face, and very much tempted to kiss her there and then, "Would you like me to take you home?"

She said quietly, "Yes," and picked her handbag up from the floor.

"I'm sorry I'm so late. Plane was horribly delayed," she heard someone say breathlessly and turned to look straight into the eyes of Jeremy who had come rushing in, still in his travelling clothes.

Nine

The Blue Paradise Café closed at 10 p.m. Five minutes before closing time, a waitress came up to them with the bill and a polite reminder. They had been sitting at the table for barely ten minutes, during which time she had managed to compose herself to have a good look at him, to see how the image of 1980 matched with that of 1984.

He was still the same, good-looking, bright-faced, high spirited person who had so attracted her. She thought she saw a new depth in his eyes, of something indefinable, and heard a new gravity, in his voice, of something not yet nameable.

As for herself, she had apparently not changed in his eyes. He had made just one observation: "You look exactly the same," and then was done with the conventions and trivialities of greeting and exchange, clearly having weightier concerns in mind.

He said, as he got up, "Let's go. Cheng Koo Street. First stop."

It was weird. It was unbelievable. He was going to enact their meeting of four years ago, down to the last detail. Cheng Koo Street, Pagoda Lane, the airport – exactly in that order. The excitement, the anticipation, the joy, then the confusion and pain of the parting – presumably in that order too. Like a movie being replayed.

Four years had elapsed during which so many things must have happened, so much living gone through, endured, enjoyed, suffered, wept over, laughed about, and here he was, four years older, a married man, probably a father, appearing in her life once more, and saying, "Let's go!" He was coolly picking up the past as if it were a yesterday, coolly tying 1980 to 1984, as if there had never been any intervening years.

What manner of madman was he, to so brazenly disregard reality and command time to a standstill for his amusement? She saw the old insouciance, the old sparkling, restless, creative spirit that had made him stand in the middle of angry traffic on Orchard Road, wildly waving a message on the palms of his hands, but was now making him run breathlessly though a tired, grey world, painting it with the bright colours of a child's untrammelled joy. If there were one pure dreamer left in a world undulled by the realities of duty and purpose and profit, it was Jeremy Matthew Lee Yu-min. He was in the world, but not of the world. He had come to her and cast a spell over her.

But that was 1980. This was 1984.

The four years had enclosed the most painful period of her life. But she had successfully made the transition from innocence to experience. She would always wonder how she had managed it. It had been a massive task – saying goodbye to her dream, putting it away from the sharp, scrutinising eyes of the world, teaching her heart to be less trusting and more wary, for its own good. She was not yet in the hard gleaming world inhabited by Kim and Suneetha and Jennie where the heart was fitted with the survival machine of the clicking abacus or calculator, of the ledger where debits on one side must be quickly offset by credits on the other. But one of these days, she expected to arrive, and then her rehabilitation would be complete. "Welcome to the real world," her friends would say with relief and delight. And her heart, before entering would turn to have a last look at the secret place where her dream had been hidden away, and bid it a last fond farewell.

Meanwhile, that heart, wary but aroused, sceptical but whetted, was ready to respond to the unfolding events of this strange day, the anniversary of that first strange day, four years ago. She faced Jeremy and asked what she had not had the temerity to do four years ago, when she was still the wide-eyed innocent: "Why?"

He brooked no whys. He was the same irrepressible blithe spirit whose boundless energy swept away all the tedious whys and hows and wherefores of conventional communication and discourse. Four years hence, and another four, and another four, he would remain the same. He would go into old age with the incorrigibility of youth.

"Let's go!" he repeated exuberantly, and she found herself in a quandary. The instinct for bold and defiant adventure, long suppressed, sprang up in joyful release; the cautiousness, stronger than the burnt child's dread, asserted itself too and warned; "The wound's hardly healed. You want to trust this man – with your heart again?"

And it was at this point that her heart forgot its own wound and remembered another's, that it had caused only a short while ago. "Jeremy, will you excuse me while I go to make a phone call. An urgent one," she said and was off in a hurry, looking for a pay phone to make a call to K.S.

She needed to speak to K.S., to say something, anything, and would be thankful if he did not hurl her words back at her and slam down the phone. She had done him a grievous wrong, and as long as it was not righted, she would not have the peace of mind or heart to concentrate her attention on this meeting with Jeremy, breathtaking in its promise of both peril and surprise. The urgency had as much to do with self interest as guilt. Once again, she was aware of her extraordinary position between the two men in her life, loved in different ways, whose paths intersected in an explosion of hostile rivalry. Plunged into a churning turmoil of excitement and remorse, she wanted to be able to separate out the emotions and deal with each separately.

K.S. was not in, or was refusing to take the call. Li-ann gave up and returned to Jeremy.

She would never forget that horrifying one minute in the café, when after a quick perfunctory handshake with Jeremy, K.S. had turned to look at her, his face taut and pale, his eyes blazing fire and saying, "Choose. Him or me. Now."

The curt finality had to do with the extreme pique of being accepted one moment and rejected the next. Those few minutes of warm togetherness and understanding when she had turned to him for comfort, and he had given it in full, loving measure, had been a turning point for him, in the long struggle to win her heart. It was the first real sign that his dream might be fulfilled at last. She had surprised herself and delighted him.

Then the next moment, his dream had smashed with the reappearance of hers. That was the nature of dreams: they played havoc with lives.

She had uttered a little cry upon seeing Jeremy. That, and the instant mobilisation of her entire body for the expression of surprise and joy, had not been lost on K.S. To make matters worse, she had lifted up a hand to touch him by way of a placating gesture, while still staring transfixed at the newly arrived visitor. He had brushed away her hand roughly and walked out of the café.

While waiting for a taxi to take them to Cheng Koo Street, she excused herself once more to make a call to K.S. There was again no reply. "Who's he? You must like him a lot," said Jeremy and showed no more interest in the rival, being bent on getting a taxi quickly.

"Some more *kuay teow* for Kai Ma?" said Li-Ann. "From Uncle Bah Bah's stall? You see, I haven't forgotten."

"That's good!" cried Jeremy. "But no. You'll see." He told her briefly that Kai Ma had died, and he had no idea whether Uncle Bah Bah was still around.

"No more than two hours to spare before the airport?" said Li-Ann. "See, I remember everything." There was a biting quality in her voice which she could not help. She thought, Yes, the tears, the pain, the callous trifling of my feelings and dreams. And yes, the crazy promise, made on a whim, and carried out on a whim. But I'm wiser this time. She would save the most important question for the last: When you made that promise, did you have any intention of keeping it?, and force him to discipline his madcap energies long enough to give a clear answer.

She would ask other questions, about himself, his family, his work, his feelings for her – yes, that, too! – and pin him down to specific answers. In 1980, her naivete had allowed him to get away with large gaps in her knowledge of him; in 1984, she would extract the necessary information with which to make a clear, sensible decision regarding themselves, she, twenty six, single, attractive, much courted, happy and successful in her career, he, thirty, married, managing some family business, living abroad. That decision had to be final. The love she had always dreamed of – pure, total, pristine – could never be hers nor his now, to give or receive. Don't come to see me anymore.

Don't feel obliged to keep a promise that was worthless in the first place.

That would be when she would not only say goodbye to her dream, but bury it. Right now, it was a dream on life support; she would hurry it to a merciful end.

Meanwhile, there was this night adventure which, despite her silent, grave deliberations and the increasing uneasiness regarding K.S., she was excitedly looking forward to. There was a piquancy about it all that was irresistible. She had no need for any anxiety, for she was in control this time A temporary suspension of reality only, her friends would say, not its forsaking. We can all tolerate that. It may even be good for the soul.

At the back of the taxi on their way to Cheng Koo Street she fell into deep introspection and was jerked out of it by something which Jeremy repeated, in a louder tone of voice. He was looking earnestly at her.

"I'm sorry! I was just so lost in my thoughts!" she said, with a laugh.

"I'd like to ask what they are."

"Not now." She thought, Not so fast. I'll give out information about myself slowly. Bit by slow bit. I've learnt that from you.

Jeremy said, looking out of the car window, "It feels so good to be back," and put his arm around her. He drew her closer to him, and laid her head on his shoulder.

A thought occurred to her, so devastating in its impact she was sure Jeremy felt the sudden tremor in her body. Contrary to her belief all this time, he was not married!

He had not spoken of a wife; his wedding ring finger remained unmarked. She stole a sideways glance at it again, on the hand pressed on her shoulder. Free of any gold or platinum band. He was as free as he was in 1980.

A replay of a movie made four years ago, but with a change in the ending. This was the second chance offered by Fate which had emerged, after the years of sheepish hiding, to make restitution. The ways of Fate in the service of this awesome thing called love were surely mysterious. She had read a story, as a child, of a little girl who wept over a sad ending in her storybook. A fairy appeared with a pair of scissors. "Cut it out," said the fairy. "But that will ruin my book!" said the little girl, who had got it for her birthday. "No, it won't," said the fairy and proceeded to help the little girl cut out the sad ending . "Throw it away, since it makes you unhappy," said the fairy and the little girl obeyed and threw it away. "Now read the story again," said the fairy, and the little girl was astonished to see a new page where the old one had been cut off, containing exactly the ending she wanted.

It was unreal, like being in another dimension of time and reality while sitting at the back of a taxi on the way to a real street called Cheng Koo Street in a real country called Singapore.

"Isn't it wonderful?" said Jeremy, and he laid his cheek against the top of her head and kissed it tenderly.

She said, "Yes," and found herself wriggling deeper into the warmth of his embrace.

Ten

Jeremy said, looking around at the food stalls with their roaring stove fires and sizzling pans, "Cheng Koo Street will never be the same again. I don't like all this urban renewal business." The food sellers didn't either; they looked glum. The mood seemed to have spread to their fires which roared less energetically, and to their pans which sizzled less appealingly than they did in 1980.

"That was Uncle Bah Bah's stall, do you remember? The fabulous *kuay teow* with its inimitable mix of garlic and cockles and lard bits." From the topic of the *kuay teow* to the person for whom he had gone to so much trouble to procure it, would be a natural step. But Jeremy never mentioned his Kai Ma, so she missed the opportunity of asking him if he had returned to Singapore for the funeral. Kai Ma, who had played so prominent a part in the scenario then, seemed to have vanished from it now. He was deftly excising bits from the past, whittling it down to a manageable piece to fit into the present.

She would ask her questions but they would not be intrusive, following naturally upon whatever references to 1980 he chose to make. She would quietly watch the unfolding of the evening of 29 February 1984, as she had the evening of 29 February 1980, and wait to see the promised difference of ending.

They sat down at one of the rough wooden tables and ordered some food "I knew it! I knew it!" exclaimed Jeremy excitedly, and he pointed to someone approaching them. "It was an uncanny feeling, but I just knew he would come to us this evening. I thought of him all the time I was in the plane."

The object of so much keen anticipation was coming straight towards them. Still in the ridiculously pretentious oriental robe and cap, the fortune-teller of 1980 waved his arms about and smiled broadly, displaying the bad teeth that had become much worse now, being no more than a few black stumps.

"You will be blessed with love all your days," he said, standing before them and bowing reverently as he spoke. "Your hearts will be filled with joy." He turned round, saw a couple at a nearby table looking on, and cried out to them, "See these two beautiful young people? I recognised them at once. I'm a useless old man now, but I remember faces I saw ten, twenty years ago!"

The old man who had brought hope to many with his predictions of huge fortunes to be made in business or the stock market and assurances of at least one male heir, ignored these usual dispensations of the gods and concentrated on love. In a thin, quavering voice he sang a paean to love, his arms stretched out in their long silken sleeves. Jeremy paid him the five dollars – over the four years, the fortune-teller had not raised his fee – and gave him another ten, when, in a sudden burst of inspiration, he took out two circlets of red thread from his robe pocket, and proceeded to put one round Jeremy's wrist and the other round Li-ann's. "Now you are bound together forever; no force in heaven or on earth can separate you," he said solemnly and bowed again.

"The old crook," said Jeremy, laughing as they left Cheng Koo Street. "The gods permit him to tell falsehoods, to make a modest living," adding, "but I'm glad he came. I knew he would. I felt it in my bones. The evening's going to be perfect."

She wondered if their next stop would be Pagoda Lane, to pay respects to Kai Ma's memory, if not her actual ghost, still lingering in the home she had occupied for so many years. The surreality of the evening was increasing by the minute. It was as if they, the fortune-teller, and all those they came in contact with, were following a script, talking and behaving with strict fidelity to it, in obedience to some large purpose still undisclosed. She thought, as she continued to stay comfortably in Jeremy's arms and looked at the taximan in front, "Perhaps he's the same taximan from 1980." There they all were – part of some strange world that had split off from the real world, and taken a life of its own.

Jeremy made the taxi stop in front of a shophouse in a little known street in Chinatown, now all boarded up, ready to be torn down, like four others in a row, to make way for new buildings.

"My birthplace," he said fondly. "Thirty years ago. In a little room on the top floor." He could not have taken her to see the Toom, even if he wanted to, the whole place being padlocked and boarded up, a sad picture of total dereliction and abandonment. He lingered in the space in front of the house, suddenly deep in thought. She watched him in the dim light of a street lamp, in a continuing sensation of calm enjoyment and wondering anticipation. The voice of caution had by now completely receded, its place taken by the eager tones of a revived hope.

Jeremy turned to her, took her hands in his and said, "I can't think of a more appropriate place than this, my birthplace, the place where I grew up, where, as a little boy, I dreamt dreams."

Appropriate for what? But she would wait patiently for the unfolding of his heart.

"Look," he said, pointing to an upstairs window, with one of the boards fallen loose and in danger of crashing down any moment. "The exact spot where I used to sit and dream dreams. I was only five, and I had a dream which has never left me."

It was a dream of love. A little boy sat by an upstairs window in a shophouse in old Chinatown, looked at the bustling life below, of honking cars and old men and women pushing carts and housewives with their shopping baskets, and dreamed, not of gleaming toys or big houses or faraway places to go to, but of being loved always. She could see the little boy vividly, with his large, pensive eyes, small fists pressed against his cheeks.

The dream had continued into adulthood. Jeremy said that he had been extremely fortunate in his youth, surrounded by people who understood and loved him, especially his Kai Ma. A life hollowed out by love's departure, or bleached by its slow withdrawal, was the saddest thing on earth.

Had he come back, all the way from Canada, after four years, to take her to this derelict spot in old Chinatown, his birthplace, to declare his love for her? He had been engaged to be married, but he realised that he loved her only and flew back to Singapore, on the anniversary of their first meeting, to pick up from where they had left. Love had come full circle, a golden, shining circle. Henceforth, the drabbest part of Chinatown would be a shining spot for her. Was this meeting the precise point where the script changed and took a different direction? This must be where 1984 would depart from 1980 and write its own ending.

A rat ran over her foot, making her scream. Then they heard a crash; the loosened board from the window had fallen down, as it had been threatening to do. "Let's go and talk over some coffee; there must be some coffeehouse still open," said Jeremy and they were off once more in a taxi. It was past midnight.

Jeremy said, as soon as they were seated at a table in The Café Royale and she had taken a quick look around and wondered about the significance of cafés in her life: "I have to tell you something. Please bear with me."

Please bear with me. This boded no good. Love needed no opening, apologies. Apologies were hateful, clouding love's pure crystal. Suddenly she was all alertness. All her faculties wound up to a trembling pitch, she prepared to listen, to catch every word and nuance of what he was going to say next.

"I am unhappy in my marriage," said Jeremy. "Was unhappy. That would be a more accurate statement. Past tense. For I have managed to overcome the pain. Because of you. You have kept me whole through all these years."

The man was impossible! In the course of less than an hour, he had made her go through wild spirals of doubt and longing, pain and hope, joy and shock. She was giddy with the effort of keeping up with her emotions, all shooting in different directions, like unruly fireworks.

She surprised herself by her calmness as she sat listening to him. The man who had been incapable of organised narrative was now taking her, slowly and carefully, on a complete journey of his heart, along the twisting paths of its pain. Once before, four years ago, she had seen the brightness of his face darken with anxiety as he saw her crying and tried to stop her tears. Now the face, in the midst of the sombre telling of lost dreams, was once again losing all brightness, the voice all cheerfulness.

Jeremy's unhappiness in his marriage had begun almost from the start, and it was because he was making Florence unhappy.

Their honeymoon in Italy had been a disaster, with Florence insisting on cutting it short, to return home. He blamed himself for his inability to make his wife happy. "I didn't understand her; perhaps I still don't," he said ruefully. "But the marriage had to work. It was a commitment, a sacred bond. I had to do something, everything, to save it." He kept blaming himself and made it seem that the responsibility of saving the marriage, in order to be commensurate with the blame, devolved entirely upon himself.

She saw Florence in her mind, a pale, intense woman with dark eyes, dark hair, crimson mouth, perfectly manicured nails, standing regally apart, looking in upon the mess with cold disdain. It was amazing how the picture, built upon the nothing he had told of her appearance, was as clear as if it had come straight from a recent photograph.

"It was horrible," he said. "I could never have imagined that a woman could be made so unhappy by a man who loved her and promised to cherish her. Or that the man could be so unhappy trying not to make her unhappy. It all became so confusing that I wasn't sure about anything anymore."

Out of the tumult of her feelings as she listened to him, one stood out in the clarity of its anger and provoked a question that she could never have uttered out loud: "Has it ever occurred to you that all this could be because you married her out of obedience and not love?" Out of the tumult too, came a thought which softened the anger, but not the pain: "Whatever his faults, this man towers over others in his simple goodness and capacity for loving."

"Then Dylan came, and I thought things would improve," said Jeremy, and he brought out his wallet and showed a picture of a little, serious-faced child with an arm around a large, friendly-looking dog. No picture of the wife. Only of the son. He spoke effusively and enthusiastically about Dylan, his eyes shining with pride and joy. They became clouded again with anxiety as he continued, "But everything became worse. And it affected Dylan's health, young though he was. Children have a way of understanding things that are lost on adults. I often found Florence crying. She said I didn't really love her. She accused me of a whole lot of things, which I need not mention here, but the recurring accusation was the most puzzling: I didn't love her. How could she say that? I had married her, was devoted to her and swore to protect and cherish her all my life."

Li-ann thought, "He's confusing marriage vows with love. He's forgetting that a woman wants a man's love, not his proving it."

"Then one day," said Jeremy, "I took a long walk by myself in the countryside. I needed to be alone, to be in touch with the purity of sky and hills and trees to think, to sort out the confusion in my mind and heart. I must have walked for hours. And then it came. I mean, the truth. It came with such force that I was almost struck to the ground! I got up and had to lean against a tree for support."

So he too had experienced the blinding flash on the way to the Damascus of his heart's truth. Li-ann thought, "I'll be patient," meaning he was taking too long to come to the part where she came in. *I think I have managed to overcome the pain because of you. You have kept me whole through all these years.* A man, bound to be faithful to one woman, was declaring his love for another. Love was committing itself to the path of risk and danger; where would it take them?

You have kept me whole through all these years. His declaration, coming from a full heart, had already become indelibly inscribed in her memory, to bring comfort or cause sorrow. If she uttered the words aloud to herself she would have to mouth them slowly, making each syllable carry its share of the portentous meaning. Everything else that he had said before or would say after would be seen and judged in the light of those words.

Eleven

Jeremy said, "All of us have our moment of awakening and truth. Mine came in the middle of a forest – I remember so clearly, how can I ever forget – when I thought I heard aloud, swooshing sound, like rushing water, and then realised that it was coming from inside me, from somewhere in the brain or heart or soul – it made no difference. The monstrous sound pounded my ears relentlessly. It was truth beating upon the gates and saying, 'Don't keep me out anymore!' And the truth was that I was dying! A dying inside, a shrivelling up of spirit, which is far worse than the death of the body. I was like a bird starved of air and wind, so that it could only fold up its wings, curl up and die. Love and joy – I needed them. A life gutted by the withdrawal of either would be unbearable. Mine had become a loveless and joyless marriage, yet still a marriage, based on a sacred promise to cherish and protect forever."

It would be both this idealistic man's pain and solace to live by absolutes: love was indestructible, marriage was indissoluble. While all around him, he could hear the deafening roar of marriages crashing to the ground, he stood by its sanctity and prepared to sacrifice the joyousness that was an essential part of his nature. It was part of his idealism to submit the crying needs of the heart to some abstract, flawed principle.

Li-ann did not know whether to consider him fool or saint. He was probably both.

"I was no saint," said Jeremy and he did not mean the solace of clandestine love. Love to him was the love sanctified by a vow, a love as open and free and innocent as the wind, untainted by guilt. "For a while, I was deeply resentful, and struggled to find a way out. I could be real mean in my frustration, like a cornered animal, ready to spring and attack. That only made things worse. My son was my sole comfort. But it was a wife's love I needed. My mother observed my pain, but I could not tell her anything. After a while, I gave up hope. Florence was away often, in connection with some family business in Hong Kong and Taiwan. Dylan, young though he was, had retreated into his own sad little world. I remember attending a play many years ago in which the last words of a dying young man were 'The sun, the sun.' He was going blind from some disease, but I think the sunlight he was calling out for was the joy of life, the zest for living. That was the light I was screaming for in those days, the darkest of my life. Light for myself, light for Dylan, light for Florence, all of us trapped in our small, dark, airless little worlds. And then one day, as I was idly gong through some things in a drawer, I found your letter."

He took out his wallet and pulled out the letter. It had been folded into a small square, but she saw the words instantly in her mind, though she had never thought of them once, scrawled so boldly, so exuberantly that day, four years ago, to challenge her dream man to come forward and make himself known. The daring invitation floated before her eyes now, in all their teasing insouciance: *There is a place I want to go to, but I don't know where; there is a person I want to meet, but I don't know whom.*

It was no more than a schoolgirl's fantasy, and it had become woven into the troubled tapestry of the man's longing.

She heard herself saying, with a little embarrassed laugh, "That was a schoolgirl's infatuation with a custom that is not known in Singapore, much less practised. St Valentine's Day is an event here; 29 February means nothing."

"But it means a lot to me!" exclaimed Jeremy. "I mean, when I first got your note, I was more amused than anything, and it provided a welcome diversion for a very dull evening. I had thought no more of it, until that day. I read it again, and then many times more, and it all came back – the joy, the vibrancy, the laughter. And then the memories of that day came streaming back. We were so alive and so happy. I can still see myself clearly, in that ridiculous pose in the middle of Orchard Road, waving my arms wildly about, with the message in lipstick. I want to be able to do that always, and for Dylan to be able to do that when he grows up – reaching out for life in its totality, embracing it whole. And I see you coming to me through dangerous traffic, so full of life and both of us on our jaunt together, through the night streets of Singapore. I did not know it then, but I had never been so happy before. And I have never been that happy since. We were celebrating life, and life was celebrating us! I thought, 'This is something I need to recapture, before it is lost forever to me.' It began as a wish, and grew into an obsession. And strangely, I thought of the funny old fortune-teller, with his predictions of love and I thought, 'I'd really like to see him again and listen to him.' Tonight, I was certain I would see him, to repossess some of the remembered joy, and I was right."

Their first 29 February encounter had become a sad reminder of what he had been, an urgent hope of what he might still be. When he shouted out that promise to her, at the last minute, he had no idea that it would be his very redemption. Born of a simple need to comfort and stop tears, it had become vow and prophecy. For, no matter what happened, he would come to Singapore every four years, on the anniversary of that luminous day, to celebrate once more the innocence and joy lived all over again, and return home to Canada, revived and recharged. That way, his spirit would not die a slow death. That way, he could go on in his marriage.

"It's something to look forward to, if nothing else," he said, "for life must be lived forward."

A spirit, denied its true unfolding, had withered, then tried to revive itself by compromises. His vow of fidelity to one woman, ironically, could be kept only through a vow he had made to another. Through an amazingly convoluted process of internalisation he had forced the two vows to co-exist and work for him. The impossible man had worked out an impossible strategy to save himself and she was part of the strategy.

In reply to her question about whether his wife knew about his present visit and intended future visits to Singapore, he would only say that he had had a very hard time convincing her about his need for it and getting her to agree at last. She had not wanted him to come to Singapore for Kai Ma's funeral, but had reluctantly agreed to this visit. It was apparently some kind of pact between them, settled on at last, in the long, arduous negotiations to save a floundering marriage.

There it was again the picture of a dark, cold, unsmiling, beautiful woman, floating back into her mind. Her imagination drew in more details – hair pulled back from a beautiful white forehead, tasteful clothes, tasteful jewellery, but an unadorned wedding finger. At some stage in their marriage, while struggling hard to preserve it, both husband and wife must have agreed to cast off its symbol.

The picture enlarged to include a scene of her playing with the small, grave-faced son, in the desultory manner of a tired, busy woman, ever away on business or on the phone for long distance business negotiations, who cannot wait for the child to be taken away by the nanny for bath or bed.

Love paints all rivals, absent or non-existent, in the darkest hues of malice.

"She thinks I'm weird," he said, and would tell her no more about his wife. This man had a natural aversion for discomfiting subjects. He told only what was necessary, his buoyant spirit fleeing the confines of harsh reality for the open spaces of imagination. He turned to her and held her hands in his. It was frightening – this investing her with a redemptive power she could not claim. Her silly little note of four years back had become a charm, an amulet, a shield against desolation and the death of the soul.

She turned cynical and thought, "A cheap little ploy, that's really what it is, to get away from an intolerable wife and a cold winter, to come flying to sunny Singapore every four years." But any cynicism melted away in the warmth of this man's overpowering sincerity and earnestness. It was a guilelessness, and a purity of spirit that had captivated and was continuing to captivate her. Even her worldly friends, locked into their cold calculations and manoeuvres would be attracted by this man.

He looked trustingly at her, this strange, exasperating, wonderful, infuriating man who had come out of her dreams and was turning her life upside down, and said, "Will you?"

If only those words of ardent need had been uttered in an earlier time, with a different meaning, before life's messiness of pain and guilt had set in. Will you? A two-word question that was a prelude to the longed for three-word declaration. If only. She realised, with a shudder, that her love for this man would always be expressed in the language of missed opportunity and futile hope.

She said, "Of course. You are always free to come to Singapore, whenever you like," and watched his face break out in its brightness again, as if her assent was all it needed to make his marriage and his life whole again.

"Your letter, my lifeline," he said putting it back in his wallet and putting the wallet back in the pocket of his trousers. "How strange, that in my darkest moment, I remembered a girl in Singapore, a thousand miles away, her wonderful note, her wonderful smile, her love of life, and knew at once she was my solace and my redemption." How strange, too, she was tempted to comment out loud, that it had never occurred to him to ask how the girl in Singapore might be feeling about all this.

She had been a diversion on 29 February 1980. She was a source of comfort, a reminder of a happier past on 29 February 1984. Would she be something different through each quartet of years until, well into the bleakness of grey hairs and dulled eyes, she woke up one morning and forced herself to say, "Enough. I've been everything, except a woman to love." While he kept his marriage alive and continued to live with and cherish another woman through the years, she would continue to live her solitary existence, and be expected, on precisely appointed dates to welcome his arrival with her gift of the solace and strength he needed, like so much water or food given to the weary traveller, who, thus recharged, goes on his way.

Jeremy had conferred upon her the unique role of being a provider of comfort, a resuscitator of hope, once every four years. In between, while she thought and worried about him, he would have no need to think or worry about her, except when it was time once more to get ready to fly to Singapore to make his rightful claims upon her.

Intolerable! Intolerable!

In 1980, all he gave her was remorse. From 1984 and onwards, it would be gratitude. She did not know which was worse.

"Li-ann, you look troubled," said Jeremy, looking worriedly at her. "Are you sure it's all right, I mean, my coming to see you every 29 February? I never consulted your feelings, selfish beast that I am! Are you sure it's okay?"

When had he ever consulted her feelings? She said with a sharpness in her voice that was difficult to conceal, "Jeremy, I thought I'd already told you that you could come to Singapore whenever you liked. Singapore is a free place. Anyone can visit, anytime."

A diversion, a comfort, an abstraction, an ideal. That was all she was to him, or could ever be. The evening could not have ended more painfully. But this time she shed no tears. She was much stronger now. And everything had become very much clearer now. She had only herself to blame. She had created a dream, given it all her love and demanded the same kind of love in return. She had forgotten that a dream had its own life, and its own dreams of love.

Jeremy insisted on taking her home. At the door, he embraced her warmly and said, pressing his lips on her forehead, "You have no idea how happy you have made me." She was aware of a slight movement of the window curtains. Her mother would be hanging around, as soon as she entered, to find out who that was and what was going on not through the insistent questions of the old days, but through a flurry of irrelevant attentions, such as bringing her ginseng tea or spotting a stain on her blouse and offering to remove it. She would, for once, be open with her mother. "That was the Dream Man," she would say. "Do you remember? The one you were going to pinch to see if he was real? Well, Mother, he is real."

She went to bed with a headache. As always, she welcomed sleep as the best balm for a confused, bruised heart. But one thing was certain. She would never see him again. Not 29 February 1988. Nor 29 February 1992.

Not ever.

Twelve

Li-ann, appointed godmother to Kim's first born well in advance of the birth, was among the first to visit the baby in hospital, in April 1985, and subsequently became most prominent guest at all the important events in the little girl's life, including a lavish First Month celebration, and a lavish First Birthday banquet at a top restaurant, for which the doting father reputedly paid a cool ten thousand.

Lynette Sim Su Lin was one of those children who could be described as a special favourite of the gods, destined from birth to a disproportionate share of beauty, intelligence and sheer irresistibility. Li-ann who at this stage of her life was resigned to a single and childless future, was ready to spoil the little god-daughter outrageously, giving in to her every demand. For from a very young age, the child had learnt to manage the adult world by a mixture of charm, guile and pure will power, having worked out in her little mind the most effective strategies of manipulation. She bawled, stamped her feet, crept up knees for a cuddle, dispensed kisses, gave out imperious orders, and reduced everyone in the household to adoring helplessness.

Lynette Sim Su Lin in 1987 was pronounced the darlingest child in Singapore; nobody could imagine then that the talkative, precocious, bright-eyed little girl would fade into the sullen, troubled teenager during the years of the parents' bitter divorce and endless squabbles.

In December 1987, Kim, then still enjoying the prosperity of her marriage, decided to celebrate Li-ann's birthday with a dinner party at home, to which The Group would be invited, together with a mysterious Mr Edward Ng whom Kim wanted Li-ann to meet. The Group was still tactfully avoiding the subject of the disastrous second encounter with the Dream Man – Li-ann had never told any of them the full story – but felt free to talk openly of those of their acquaintances whom she might be interested in meeting. In 1987, all in the group had got married to the men they were dating in 1984, and all seemed contented enough in their marriage, and anxious that Li-ann should join them in that happy state. She was going to be twenty nine years old, already three years in the danger zone of lonely spinsterhood so feared by her mother.

Mrs Chang had given up all efforts at matchmaking, after Li-ann in 1986 refused to meet one Mr Chow Leung Liu, a cousin of a cousin, and a prosperous businessman in Hong Kong. Not having entirely lost her sense of humour in these matters, Li-ann told her mother she was rejecting Mr Chow on the basis of his possession of a gold tooth, just as she had rejected a certain prosperous financier, years back, on the sole basis of his inability to speak correct English. Her mother had said, "I really don't know what to do with you."

"All right," said Li-ann to Kim. "You go ahead and invite Mr Big Nose Edward Ng to my birthday dinner." The reference to that feature was for the benefit of the little god daughter perched on her lap and listening intently, as usual, to adult conversation. Kim, when asked to describe the guest's appearance, had rather apologetically mentioned a large, bulbous nose which should not, she said emphatically, detract from the appeal of his very sizable fortune.

Turning to the god-daughter still perched on her lap, Li-ann said, with all the seriousness of face and voice that she could muster, "Now Lynette, I want you to listen very carefully to me. Your mummy will be very generously celebrating my twenty ninth birthday for me. That means there will be twenty nine candles on the cake. They will make me a very old person. So you mustn't tell anyone that your Godma is twenty nine years old. You promise?" Lynette nodded.

For the rest of the day, the little girl went about solemn-faced with the weightiness of the secret.

On the evening of the birthday dinner, the first guest to arrive was Mr Edward Ng. His entry must have coincided precisely with the moment when the weight had become too great to be borne any longer, for Lynette rushed to him, announcing shrilly, "My godma is NOT twenty nine, you know!"

The second discharge of a little heart unfairly burdened with the keeping of too many adult secrets came moments later, when she stood in front of Mr Ng, looked up at him and asked, with great interest, "Why is your nose so big?" Li-ann hurried up to extend a quick apology and to scoop up the little girl into her arms for a laughing hug and kiss.

In the old days, Mrs Chang, looking at Li-ann playing so delightedly with a child, might have been provoked to remark with sly, maternal malice, "You would be playing with one of your own, if you weren't so choosy and so fixed on that stupid Dream Man." Nowadays, much cowed, but with her anxieties for her daughter's future by no means diminished, she expressed them only in a roundabout way and waited patiently for a suitable opening in their conversation to slip in a hint or two.

At the beginning of January 1988, Li-ann did a review of the major events in her life, since that second meeting in 1984.

They did not amount to much; there was none that could be remotely described as a milestone. In the middle of 1985, she had been given a promotion in her work in the junior college and made Head of the English and Literature Department; in 1986, she had gone on a brief tour of China with her mother; in the same year, she had gone on a conducted tour of Europe; in 1987, she had enrolled for a Chinese painting course at the YMCA which she found very relaxing, and had toyed with the idea of writing a book, possibly a collection of short love stories. In that year too there had been a scare: her mother had been diagnosed with breast cancer and undergone a mastectomy, from which, fortunately, she appeared to have recovered amazingly, going straight from the operating to the mahjong table, as she liked to joke to her friends.

At the beginning of January 1988, too, Li-ann received a postcard from K.S. He was living in London, and working in an architects' firm. Since that dreadful day on 29 February 1984, when he had stormed out of the Blue Paradise Café, Li-ann had not heard from him. She fretted for a while, missing his visits very much. His mother, who apparently knew of the shabby treatment of her son, had coldly informed her, after numerous, persistent calls that K.S. was no longer in Singapore, and would she please stop calling.

The guilt had remained through the years, a small insistent voice of reproach, sometimes surfacing as a troubled dream. It was a guilt that was not unmixed with a certain gratifying sense that he could love her so much. But it was slowly fading away, and just when she thought she was free of it at last and that her friendship with K. S., like so many other things, could be relegated to the sad dust heap of memory, the postcard came. In the almost undecipherable scrawl of a person not used to writing or fond of it, the postcard said: "I'll be back in Singapore for a week, beginning 4 January. Could I see you? I'll call first," followed by a signature recognisable only to herself.

Li-ann could not help a wry smile. The men in her life asked to see her, on such and such a day, in such and such a year, leaving no return address, as if they assumed her answer could never be: "Please don't come. Please don't upset the even tenor of my life. I have just learnt to be on my own and to rather like it."

She was not sure she wanted to see K.S. again. She searched her heart for any remnant of fondness, found only the guilt of that dreadful, shabby treatment, and then began to look forward to the visit to make the long-awaited apology. Another postcard arrived soon afterwards. "You'll do me a great favour by not referring to any past incident – you know what I mean. So no apologies."

So he, too, wanted to expunge the past from his life, to clean the heart out of all bitter memories. As if it could ever forget. Of course she would co-operate fully. Did he want a fresh start? Had he heard about the sad ending to the foolish little foray of her heart, and believing it to be now permanently chastened and humbled, was once more trying to pick up from where he had left off? Hope lies eternal in the human breast; hope was now breaking its silence and returning to express itself once again. How would she react, after all this while?

She actually ran to meet him when the doorbell rang, and was taken aback when not one, but two persons presented themselves. K.S. said, "Li-ann, meet Jocelyn, my fiancée." She said, "Hi, Jocelyn, so pleased to meet you," as if it was the most natural thing in the world for a woman, at one moment, ready to fling her arms round an old, faithful, devoted admirer, and at the next, to shake hands amicably with the woman who was now claiming his admiration and devotion. For as long as she remembered, there had been no other woman in K.S.'s life; he had been so deeply in love with her, so single-mindedly in pursuit of her, that she had grown accustomed to the monopoly of this good man's heart. Now she was looking at a woman who had first claim of it.

"Hey, what's this? No hug for an old buddy?" said K.S and swept her into his arms, while Jocelyn stood by, smiling. She saw it all now – the request to her in the postcard not to refer to the past, the reference to the engagement in the introduction itself, in case she forgot the request and said something potentially damaging in front of the fiancée, the pointed but casual reference to her as a buddy and therefore entitled to any number of innocuous hugs and kisses even in the fiancée's presence – a carefully planned pattern of disengagement from that part of his past that he had shared with her. She felt tears coming into her eyes, and was not sure whether it was the sense of loss felt by a vain woman superseded by another in a good man's affections, or the disappointment that could only be expressed in a refrain pounding in her brain: "This is not the K.S. I knew."

He appeared very happy. He was genuinely pleased to see her, taking her hand to hold in his several times in the course of their conversation. In full cooperation with his desire to avoid any reference to the past which might be offensive to his fiancée, who was watching both of them like a hawk, while smiling serenely all the while, Li-ann adroitly channelled all her questions along safe paths. She thought, "I don't like the woman at all," disliking especially the quick, little darts of Jocelyn's eyes, the tiny fixed smile around her mouth, her small gestures of possession and territoriality such as gently picking a piece of lint from K.S.'s sleeve, or making fussy adjustments to his collar.

"You haven't yet asked us how we met," said Jocelyn with a radiant smile, as she sat closer to K.S. on the sofa, and laid a delicate hand on his lap, the diamond engagement ring flashing a warning. "K.S., tell Li-ann how we met." Each time she felt the annoyance of being left out, as when K.S. and Li-ann talked animatedly about common friends, she moved in and waved the flag of proprietorship: "He's mine. Clear off."

Li-ann thought, "I don't want to see her again. Not even for K.S.'s sake."

At the door, before they said goodbye, Jocelyn said airily, "Did you know what K.S., stands for? You never told anybody, did you, Kit Sing?" She turned to face Li-ann, beaming with the pure joy of having scored over a rival. "'Kissing Kit Sing', that's my new name for him!" She laughed merrily. Li-ann winced.

Piqued vanity had need to vent itself. As soon as they left, her mother, who had, in the few minutes of serving drinks to the guests been observing a great deal, came out to say, "I don't think much of that girl, all artificiality and pretence," and she was quick to agree, "You're so absolutely right She's repulsive, not at all the person I imagine would make K.S. happy."

But K.S. was genuinely happy. She could see that. He saw her a few more times after that, on his own, sensing an antagonism between the two women which did not in the least disturb him, being very much in love with one and knowing he had got over the other. He did not tell Li-ann much about his years in London, but she knew that his new friends had managed to coax him out of his old unhappy, defiant self and inducted him fully into their carefree, pleasurable life. He had met Jocelyn at a party, they had begun seeing each other regularly, and one day he realised he was in love with her. The heart abhors a vacuum. Emptied of all hope for the old love, it soon found a new.

Li-ann longed to ask, when she saw K.S. again for coffee, without the fiancée being present, "Did you think of me in London? Was there any time you wanted to write to me or call me?", her own heart hating its vacuum and crying for it to be filled with anything resembling love – the affection for a cute little god-daughter, tender remembrance from somebody who had gone away and come back.

K.S., who was far more communicative than she had ever known him to be, said, "I thought very much of you at the beginning. The anger was still very great. But distance was what I needed. Distance and time. Gradually the pain disappeared, with the work, the friends, the travelling. I never did so much travelling in my life. And then I met Jocelyn." He went on talking happily, a taciturn, wry man transformed by love.

"Flee, flee," Li-ann almost wanted to scream at him. "Flee from that woman. She's not worthy of you. It's not spite talking, it's the true concern of a friend who is all the more concerned now because she had let you down." Then she wanted to scream at herself, "Come down from that high ground of faked nobility. You're just plain annoyed because you never thought K.S. would love anybody else."

Wary of postcards, she was not prepared for the one that arrived from Canada on 1 February 1988. Her heart jumped at the sight of the postmark that said 'Vancouver'. How had he managed to get her address? They had parted at her door that evening of 29 February four years ago, without any exchange of addresses. Unless of course, he had noted the number on the door and the street name as they alighted from the taxi.

Then she saw her mistake. She should have been alerted to it by the fine handwriting, certainly too delicate and neat to be a man's. It said, "My name is Florence. You know who I am. I will be at the Singapore Airport on 8 February on my way to Hong Kong. I will be in transit for some hours, and would be extremely grateful if you could come and see me then. Will you do me this favour? It is very important to me."

Thirteen

Her imagination had attached a pale intense, haughty face to the name, and thereafter embellished it with details – dark hair pulled back from an elegantly smooth and severe brow, dark eyes, a hard crimson mouth. Her imagination had gone on to attach a slender, long-limbed body to the face, a body made for lying on silken couches in an atmosphere of high passion and intrigue in the old days, and for high-powered jet-setting in designer suits and expensive perfume in the new.

During the years when she had struggled to banish him forever from her memory, the image of his wife, very strangely, had persisted, always a cold presence in the background looking in. "She accused me of not loving her," he had confided in anguish. "How could my wife say that when I had promised to love and cherish her always?" She had sometimes thought of him and his wife in the intimate darkness and softness of the marriage bed: how did they express their love and desire, this strange man and woman whose marriage seemed to have come apart during the honeymoon itself? He had also confided to her his intense love for his son, and his hope that a little boy would be the saving bridge between his hopelessly estranged parents. Could a man love a woman simply because she was the mother of his son?

Through all the images, Florence had been a tall, domineering, coldly supercilious, compellingly beautiful presence.

Now, in the airport, at a café table sitting opposite her, Li-ann saw how her imagination, generous though it was in bestowing beauty, had missed the reality by a wide margin. For Florence was an extraordinarily beautiful woman, with that kind of beauty that made passers-by instantly turn to have a second, a third look. It was not the beauty of a carefully cultivated hauteur, of skilfully applied lipstick, mascara, rouge, of expensive clothes tailored to highlight a perfect figure, but a gift that some might describe as rare, even ethereal, which the hand of time will touch but gently, so that even in old age, the woman remains beautiful and compels attention.

Fashion and beauty magazines sometimes run pictures of The Perfect Face, a composite of the best features taken from various movie star faces.

Florence could contribute several features, notably her eyes and mouth. Li-ann had never seen so much pure beauty. She could not stop staring at Florence.

But her imagination had been totally correct about the cold severity.

As soon as they sat down at the café table, Florence took out a cigarette from a pack in her handbag, lit it, then began to survey Li-ann with cool interest. "So this is the girl," she said, and let out a short, sharp laugh. Li-ann was instantly annoyed. She stood up and said angrily, "I have not come here to be subjected to any ridicule." She picked up her handbag and was getting ready to leave, when Florence stopped her with a desultory wave of her hand. "Oh, stay, for goodness' sake," she said, in a voice that suddenly sounded very tired. "I told you I needed to see you about an important matter. I'm sure you can guess."

"I have no idea what you are talking about, Mrs Lee," said Li-ann.

"Call me 'Florence' for goodness' sake, and sit down," she said, waving Li-ann back to her chair.

She turned her long slender neck this way and that, pressing and rubbing it gently, to relieve it of the tiredness of the long flight. A man who was passing by, turned to look, noticing her extraordinary beauty.

Li-ann sat down again, and tried to be calm, as thoughts raced madly through her mind. A very important matter? Jeremy's wife of eight years, whom he loved enough to resort to all kinds of weird devices to save the marriage, wanted to meet up urgently with her, to tell her something? Tell, warn, beg, plead, denounce? How much had he told his wife about her? Had it anything to do with the bizarre promise to come to Singapore to see her every 29 February? The third visit was due very soon.

She was determined to be in control. It would be intolerable for both husband and wife to come into her life to wreak damage.

Florence said, "Just what is it about 29 February that obsesses my husband? Why is he so bent on keeping such an insane promise? We've had so many rows over that. There must be something to it all. You will tell me what it is all about."

The woman was intolerably rude and presumptuous. Li-ann said, flushed with anger, "I will do no such thing." She could have got up there and then and left the insufferable woman, but she stayed, longing to hear more.

Florence said, drawing slowly on her cigarette, "He must be in love with you. That's the only logical explanation. It would not be beyond my husband, mad and unpredictable and strange as he is, to express his love for another woman in this insane manner. It would have been better for him to tell me straight to my face, 'I don't love you anymore', and go out and have an affair. I could cope with that better. Instead of which, he has this compulsion to see his lover once every four years, meantime annoying me with his looking forward so eagerly to the event. He tries not to show it, but nothing escapes me. He is obsessed with you! Are you lovers?" she demanded suddenly.

"I refuse to say anything that you are likely to use against your husband or myself," said Li-ann in a rage. "How dare you, Mrs Lee, ask me to come to see you on a so-called important matter, then insult and abuse me?"

"I'm not insulting or abusing you, and it's an important matter. For goodness' sake, sit down. I need to tell you something." Li-ann sat down again. Florence said calmly, "We have separated. A divorce is inevitable. Jeremy's very upset, and is in a confused and very vulnerable state. Somebody is out to take advantage of this and nab him quickly. She's Dylan's teacher, who gives a bad name to her profession, for she eyes the handsome fathers as they come to pick up their kids, single fathers or about-to-be-divorced fathers, ready for the picking. A real bitch. The woman has singled out Jeremy and is cunningly working on his love for his son, to entice him to her bed and the marriage registry."

Florence told her about an incident in which, one morning, she had gone to her son's school to pick him up and had seen Jeremy and the woman talking together, with Dylan between them. She was about to take Dylan away – it was her turn at the school, and clearly Jeremy had forgotten or chosen to forget that – when the bitch actually had the audacity to block her way, and then to stand very close to her husband and son, almost touching them, as if to announce to the world that they already belonged to her.

The woman. The bitch. Florence disdained to give her a name. She ground her cigarette angrily on a small saucer and said, "This I must say about my husband. He may be weird and weak and exasperatingly idealistic, but he is a good man, sterling stuff. Beside him, most men are the pits. Right now, he's all confused and vulnerable and that woman knows it. I know everything that's going on. I have ways of finding out things. And in spite of the confusion and the mess, he's bent on keeping this strange 29 February rendezvous with you. And you tell me there's nothing between you? Would you like a coffee?"

The woman was amazing. In one speech made in her beautifully modulated voice, she had told the whole story of the devastation of her marriage, praised and disparaged her husband, condemned one rival, tried to lure another into some damning confession, and then offered coffee. "Sit down, for goodness' sake," she said for the fourth time, and then called a waitress.

Li-ann thought to herself, "Be careful. Be very careful. This woman is out to destroy everyone her husband is connected with." Right now, she could not think very clearly, but already numerous things were firmly lodged in her head, for later reflection and rumination. One of them stood out in all its tantalising power: *He's obsessed with you.* The heart had thrilled to the words, only to be rebuked and warned by the head, "Don't let it happen all over again. This time it could be much worse. You can't risk any more bruising. You know that."

Florence said, looking straight into her eyes, "You know, I like you better than that bitch. I want you, when Jeremy next comes to see you, which will be very soon, to work on him too

– the best way is through his son, whom he'll die for – so that he'll marry you instead of that bitch."

She could hardly believe what she was hearing. The woman, a total stranger, was virtually giving her the order to take her husband.

"Take my advice. Jeremy is somebody worth fighting for. But I gave up the fight long ago. I know he doesn't love me. Perhaps he's never loved me. But," and here Florence let out a defiant puff of cigarette smoke, "it doesn't matter now. There's somebody who does. We'll be married soon." The hard lines on her face softened with some tender recollection of the lover.

The woman had discharged all the necessary information, condemnation, warning and advice, and was ready to go. She stood up and said, "Thank you for coming. I'm much obliged." She picked up her cigarette lighter from the table, and took a last look at Li-ann. "You're pretty," she said, smiling for the first time. "And presumably good and fun and full of life and idealistic and all that. That's Jeremy's kind of woman. Good luck to him and you."

It occurred to Li-ann to ask a question. "Does Jeremy know about our meeting today?"

Florence said, "Of course not. You wouldn't tell him, would you?"

Li-ann thought, "I have no wish ever to see her again," turned abruptly and walked away.

Fourteen

The trouble was that 29 February 1988 was a half day at the junior college, a reward for the staff and students for winning a prestigious national sports award three years in a row. A half day meant that she could keep herself occupied for only part of the long stretch of time leading to eight o'clock. Eight o'clock had settled in her consciousness as both witching and fatal hour. 'Upon the stroke of midnight' heralded many a breathtaking tale. For her, the suspense would begin at a harmless, nondescript hour when people, not bothered by dreams, ate their dinner or got ready for the family's TV time together.

Eight o'clock in the year 1988 for her was fraught, three times over, with more peril than promise. In the tumult that had rushed into her life, like a powerful current, since that first 29 February meeting, she had become superstitious, looking for meaning and significance in signs, to anchor hope in the swirling uncertainties.

Lunch with The Group – that should take her to two o'clock at least. Then some after-lunch shopping with Kim who was a compulsive shopper, buying things she did not care for, with money she had no real use for, to fill her vast cupboards, to fill an emptiness that was beginning to show in little hints dropped about her husband's secret forays in Hong Kong. But when shopping, Kim forgot all her troubles. She laughed and joked with all the boutique shop assistants, drawing attention to an expanding waistline that would no longer take the slinky dresses held out to her. Kim could always be depended upon to kill time, at least two whole hours. That would leave about three more. She might go back with Kim and play with the little goddaughter who always had new toys to show. Then back home. She would allow herself an hour and a half to soak in the tub, do her hair, face, nails, iron her dress, get ready slowly, without hurry.

In the end, Li-ann abandoned the planned programme of time management. It would serve little purpose, as no amount of frenzied physical activity would distract her from the thoughts that kept swirling around in her head, like buzzing insects impossible to quieten down. In the end, she came home from school, had a quick lunch, then locked herself in her room, lay down on her bed, and allowed her thoughts and feelings, all this while kept under strict guard, to break loose.

They broke free, a fearful flood undammed, overwhelming her, tossing her upon huge, heaving waves.

'In all the mess and confusion, he's bent on keeping his rendezvous with you. And you say there's nothing between you?' She would have rejoiced at the purest proof of a man's love his own wife's reluctant admission of it. But there had been no reluctance on Florence's part. Indeed, she had offered proof abundantly and indecently, not from the need for truth but from the desire to use one hateful rival to destroy the other, even more hateful one. Go for my husband, she had said. I don't care for your happiness or his, but I care for the pleasure of destroying someone I hate more than either of you. For Florence, revenge yielded a greater

dividend of pleasure than anything else.

Li-ann thought, "Why am I getting involved in the messiness in other people's lives? Why can't they leave me alone?" But she knew deep down she did not want one person to leave her alone. One person in the world stood out, whose destiny was ineluctably, irrevocably tied to hers. Could thoughts and feelings fly across vast seas and continents to connect, like long threads, thin, invisible but strong? If his mind dwelt as much upon her as hers on him, their thoughts and feelings about each other would by now have formed a dense and massive rope, impossible to sever. Did he dream of her, too, at night, as he lay in sleep? Her dreams of him were too numerous to tell.

It was better, according to a certain belief, for separated lovers to have bad dreams of each other than good ones, for the worse the dream, the better the reality, in obedience to some strange cosmic principle of compensation and fairness. Thus a man or woman could wake up from a nightmare and be comforted.

She had dreamt of them both, parting in tears, lost and separated from each other in dense traffic on a road, lost and separated again in the hurrying crowds at an airport and in the dank darkness of a shuttered shophouse in Chinatown. She had awakened each time, frightened and panting to face, not the promised comfort, but an even darker reality: he was far away in a distant land, and even further away in his self imposed exile of fidelity to a woman he no longer loved. The promise of 29 February, so ardently made, had meant nothing, for the few hours spent with her, every four years, were mere crumbs from love's table.

But now it could mean something. Li-ann pressed her hands against her ears and said, "Stop, stop," for hope, dangerously revived, was beating not only in her heart but at her ears, in the words uttered by his wife, which had become a deafening roar. *He's obsessed with you.* Obsession. Love. Passion. Dream. They were all the same because they nurtured and resuscitated hope, which should be totally distrusted, because it so easily flipped over and became despair.

"No, no," said Li-ann desperately. But as the minutes ticked closer to eight o'clock, her heart said "Yes." More than anything, a heart hates a vacuum. Let anything rush in – anger, fear, disappointment, hate, sorrow. Anything is more bearable than the numbing emptiness, the frightening, echoing, hollow chamber.

At seven, the phone rang, and she jumped. It could be him. He could be calling from Vancouver to say he had changed his mind about coming to Singapore after all. His wife could have told him of their meeting, twisting and distorting things to suit a new purpose, whatever it was.

She picked up the phone tremblingly, and was relieved to hear a small, tearful voice. "Godma," cried Lynette. "Boy Boy's biting me again." Lynette called at least a dozen times a day, to report the misdeeds of her small, two-year-old brother who bit her, pulled her hair, tore off her doll's arm. She calmly and stoically sat through the outrage, then flew off crying to the adults for sympathy.

"Never mind, sweetie. Just don't go near him. Tell me what you did in school today." This was good strategy. The little girl's detailed recounting of her day at the Raffles Star Kindergarten which she would have to listen very carefully to, in order to pass the comprehension test that Lynette invariably conducted through some shrewd questioning afterwards, would force her to keep her thoughts collected, her heart calm.

"Godma, you're not listening!"

"Of course I am, sweetie."

"Godma, Mommy says you have a Dream Man. He's real bad. What's a Dream Man, Godma?"

Out of the mouths of babes.

At half past seven, the sky darkened and the rain came down in torrents. "Goodness, Li-ann, where are you going?" said her mother in alarm. "It's pouring!"

The regularity of the 29 February outing had never occurred to Mrs Chang, because of the long four-year interval which in any case was always too crowded with events for recollection of any single one. But the feverish brightness in her daughter's eyes and the pale intensity on her face brought back memories. Mrs Chang repeated, "It's pouring," and added, "perhaps you should wait for the rain to stop."

Wait for the rain to stop? By now, she knew that nothing would stop her. She would wade through churning flood waters and dash through roaring flames to be in time for her appointment. That was it – an appointment only, and no more. Like him, she had become a slave to the tyranny of a strange promise that had, over the years, assumed a life of its own. Same day, same place, same time. It had become a stern commandment, carved in stone, and they had become both its keepers and its victims, for it to unload upon them whatever it chose, of pain or joy, hope or despair, love or its obverse, hate. She would go, as usual, unresisting, ready for anything.

Fifteen

In the years to come, the recollection of their calmness, approaching a perfect serenity, at this, their third and most portentous meeting, would still cause surprise.

There she was, shaking the rain out of her umbrella, and there he was, wiping it off his jacket, neither looking at the other, both meticulously going through the motions of a small, mundane, everyday act, as if, to delay, as long as possible, the moment of facing each other, looking into each other's eyes and saying: "For the first time, we are meeting as free man and woman, unshackled by anxiety and guilt. What do we do now?"

The rainwater having been got rid of, they still had to look for something to do or say, the more inconsequential the better, to prepare for an evening that both knew would have tremendous consequences on their lives thereafter.

Li-ann looked at the many people who had come into the café to take shelter from the rain, and said one or two things about them; Jeremy happened to see a large wall-dock which he said he had not noticed before, and made a comment on it. They jumped upon the topic of what had changed and what had not in the Blue Paradise Café, a subject that had so conveniently presented itself, and between them, enumerated the entire list:

new coat of paint, old furniture, old floor tiles, new plastic flowers, new menu that included, ambitiously, lobster bisque.

Jeremy said, not looking at Li-ann: "I should tell you this: Florence and I have separated. We're going to be divorced very soon."

She did not say, "I know. She told me." Instead she said, as she would say routinely to any friend who made that announcement, "I'm sorry."

Jeremy said, "What strange creatures we are. I had thought divorce was unthinkable, the greatest violation of the most deeply sacred thing we know, the worst thing that could happen to anyone. Yet when Florence told me she wanted a divorce, I experienced something akin to joy. It was a very strange feeling, a buoyancy that lifted me up, an unbearable lightness of feeling. It was as if an enormous weight around my neck, a gigantic albatross, had dropped off and sunk into the sea. I'm ashamed to admit it, but it's true. Guilt and joy – how can they co-exist?"

Li-ann wanted to say, "Throw off the guilt. You've carried it around for too long. You were made for life and joy."

He said, "Florence has generously agreed that Dylan should come to me," and again Li-ann resisted uttering aloud the rejoinder: "She mentioned the lover she's going to marry. She'll have no time for the son."

Get him. Work on his love for his son, Florence had advised her, eyes narrowing with malicious intent. But she would never do that. Their love for each other, born in an apocalyptic moment on a magical day eight years ago, would always be direct and spontaneous and full, never mediated by any third person, man, woman, or child, never re-routed along any other path.

Having done with the information, Jeremy looked

enormously relieved. A slight flush came to his face and spread to his ears and neck. He said, without looking at her, but reaching to hold her hands in his: "You have no idea how much I was looking forward to this meeting."

He had been looking forward to the meetings, every four years, under the massive self-delusion that he was going to save his marriage by saving his dream, never realising that his wife, with her hard, unillusioned stare, had seen through it all, concluded that it was really his dream that mattered most to him, and released him.

Li-ann calmly looked at this man who had reached her at last through the tortuous labyrinth of his unrealistic ideals, and could now afford to take the direct, straight path that his loving, open heart had always needed. No more the cruel interval of four years enjoined by the guilt and confusion of the past, but the joyous frequency of meeting and union, that was every lover's right. The prospect was so heady that Li-ann, for a moment, had to steady herself against the table.

She wondered, from what his wife had told her, about the bruising of that generous, loving heart, in its way out of the labyrinth.

She loved him! *I need you. I can't live without you.* Love's clichés had become stark realities: she knew, with a shuddering certainty, that life would be impossible without him.

He said, still holding her hands and looking at her: "You're beautiful." Now he was talking like the lover, not the confidante or soulmate who had kept within safe boundaries and who, when the time came for them to say goodbye, had given her only a chaste kiss on the forehead. She was certain – how her heart sang with joy! – that before the evening was over, he would kiss her deeply and passionately and declare his love unequivocally.

This man who had compared himself to a bird, was born for joy and exultation, and she was witnessing his bursting forth and soaring high up into the blue sky of a new, liberating embrace of life.

He said, "Do you remember – ?" He looked around the café, and pointed out the various spots that they ought to remember from their first wondrous encounter, even if the café disappeared in a heap of rubble – the exact spot of their table (it was amazing how, at each meeting, the table remained vacant, as if awaiting them), the spot where the little Indian boy had stood, bearing the note, the spot where the waitress had stood, when he had gone to borrow her lipstick. He had pruned off the bitter parts of memory, as no longer relevant to their present state.

Having exhausted the items of remembrance inside the café, he wanted to look for those outside it. He got up and made her get up and walk with him to the front of the café facing the road. There, he said excitedly pointing with his finger, showing her the exact spot where he had stood with the lipsticked message, a lunatic in the midst of astonished motorists, cyclists, pedestrians, shoppers.

"You never told me where you hid yourself to watch me," he said. "Show me now." She looked but could not locate the spot, the whole area having undergone massive reconstruction. A tall hotel had sprouted up where she thought the Indian man's newspaper stall had been, that had given her the idea for the 29 February message.

And still the joyful reminiscence continued, as if he had need of it, to confirm his new happiness.

She said, "Are you going to do Cheng Koo Street again? Not that you'll recognise it anymore. All the food-stalls are gone."

He said, "No. Tonight, I want us to stay put at the spot that is dearest of all, because it started it all."

The spot that started it all. The innocuous pronoun 'it', containing the whole story of their love which, before the evening was over, would have to be clearly expressed, love being a narrative with a proper beginning, middle and end. They had done with the tumultuous beginning, and should be moving towards the richness and depth of the middle, and finally, the profound fulfilment of the conclusion. She had waited long enough.

They heard strains of music coming from the hotel where the newspaper stall had been, and craned their necks to see what, in the semi-darkness outside, appeared to be part of a wedding crowd, men and women in their best clothes, talking and laughing, a photographer moving among them. "'Rasa Sayang Hotel'," read Jeremy, squinting to read the bold letters in red and white on top of the four-storey hotel. "I know what it means. 'The Feeling of Love Hotel'."

He turned to Li-ann, his face suddenly animated with exciting purpose.

"Let's go join the wedding party."

"No, we won't. We aren't guests."

"Yes, we will. Come along! It'll only be for a short while. I promise I won't do anything bad."

It was, the Jeremy she had seen in 1984, daring, bold, bursting with life's zest and energy and joy.

They entered the hotel, and moved easily among the wedding guests. The bride and groom who were standing on a stage were a very young-looking couple; they had clearly broken out of the bounds of decorum and propriety enjoined upon wedding couples in a public place, for they were singing lustily, cheered on by their rambunctious guests, while their elders, in their staid suits and *cheongsams* looked on with benign indulgence.

Li-ann stole a glance at Jeremy. He had accepted a drink from somebody, and was clapping and cheering. She had never seen him so happy. The most rambunctious of the guests, a fat young man who was clearly a little drunk, suddenly jumped up on to the stage, stood beside the bridal couple, and proposed a game. "The groom must kiss the bride," he yelled, "and every one of the male guests must follow suit. Grab your partners, gentlemen! Kiss them! The one who kisses most passionately and lovingly gets a prize. A real good prize! XO brandy! I'll be the judge!" The fat young man waved the bottle of brandy in the air, then jumped down from the stage.

The elderly guests smiled and shook their heads in amused resignation to the wild ways of the young. The bolder among the young guests were already moving towards their partners, in readiness for the competition. One man who had a moustache grabbed a young, long-haired girl in a mauve taffeta dress and kissed her boisterously. She gave a little shriek, broke away, and covered her face with her hands, laughing all the while. There was loud cheering and clapping.

"C'mon, what are we waiting for," said Jeremy, and pulled Li-ann into his arms. He kissed her deeply and passionately, only pausing at one point to hold her even closer to him, and press his face in her hair. He said something which she could not hear, for there was a roaring din in her ears as she clung to him.

The absurdity of it all would only occur to her later – the sealing of their dream with a kiss in a public place, at a wedding party which they had outrageously gatecrashed.

Jeremy felt a tap on his shoulder and turned round to see the fat young man who had started it all, brandishing the bottle of brandy in his face. "You win!" he roared, handing the prize to Jeremy, and giving Li-ann a knowing wink. "Everyone, please applaud the winners!"

There was deafening applause, hoots, wolf-whistles. Somebody shouted, "Let's have it again!" and Jeremy, turning to Li-ann and holding her as if his life depended on it, obliged once more.

Sixteen

Places became dear through their association with events, Orchard Road through those joyfully waving arms, calling out to her "Okay! Please come to me!", and now the Rasa Sayang Hotel through a kiss.

Amidst a noisy wedding crowd, they disengaged, looked at each other and became a world unto themselves, a cosmology of two. The kiss, part of a silly competition, had put the seal of legitimacy upon a dream, and enabled them to say triumphantly to a capricious Fate, "Now don't you play tricks on us anymore."

It was time for them to leave, and still they stayed, their arms around each other, intent on prolonging this moment of supreme happiness. They looked smilingly at the bridal couple descending the stage, the groom helping the bride manage her billows of tulle and lace. It was part of the evening's surreality that Li-ann, looking upon a radiant young girl suddenly thought of a tired-looking, untidily-dressed woman, some years hence, with one child on her hip and another by the hand, quarrelling noisily with her husband over money and in-laws and the dereliction of marital responsibility, and the woman would sob, and the man might respond with his own bitter cry, "What happened to the girl I married? What happened to our dream?"

Li-ann thought, "No, no," meaning that the happiness of the hour, for both herself and the bride, should tolerate no invasion of rude reality. "No, no," she said to her imagination, and reined it in from the unruly direction it was always taking.

"Let's go," said Jeremy. But the evening conspired to delay their presence at the Rasa Sayang Hotel yet further. An old man, probably not a wedding guest, but some down-and out wanderer about town looking for good things to be had, stopped him at the entrance and pointed to the bottle of brandy in his hand. The man who was old and shabby-looking, said something in an unfamiliar dialect, repeatedly pointing to the bottle and smiling. Clearly, it was not an offering of congratulations from a friendly stranger who had witnessed the merry kissing competition and the winning of the grand prize, but a daring plea. The man's gestures said boldly: "Give it to me. It means nothing to you. You can afford all the XOs in the world."

Quickly shifting his position to block out the vagrant from the view of any wedding guest who might be looking on, Jeremy gave him the prize. But he changed his mind almost immediately afterwards, and took the bottle of brandy back. "Here," he said with some embarrassment to the astonished man, pushing a small wad of money into his hands. Then he hurried away, dragging Li-ann with him to cross the road quickly, before the traffic lights turned red again.

Making their way back into the Blue Paradise Café, they witnessed a scene, not of love's celebration but of its approaching end. For a young couple, standing beside a parked motorcycle in front of the café, their crash helmets still on, were arguing loudly with each other. Soon the young man and his companion, a girl with long hair and wearing a mini skirt began shouting at each other, their bodies taut with hostility. Li-ann and Jeremy then saw the quick flash of a raised hand, heard a scream and saw the girl fall backwards and trying to steady herself

"Did you see that?" screamed the girl, and swung round to address anyone who might be near. She saw Li-ann and Jeremy and screamed again, "Did you see that? He slapped me! The bastard slapped me!"

Jeremy moved forward quickly and stood facing the young man who had fallen into a sullen silence, his long arms hanging by his side. "Look, you mustn't… Why don't you…" Jeremy did not know what else to say, and looked rather foolish.

"Oh, he's nothing but a bastard," said the girl with spirit. Suddenly she looked tired. She walked back to the parked motorcycle, got up on the pillion, adjusted her helmet, and turned to shout at the young man, "What are you waiting for?" He sprang up, evidently very relieved, and hurried back to her, mounting the motorcycle expertly. They went roaring off into the night once more.

"Well! Well!" exlaimed Jeremy laughing. his head. He said to Li-ann, "What do you make of it?" Before she could say anything, an elderly man came out of the café and stood before them. He said, shaking his head and chuckling, "Happens every time. I know. I see them very often. Fight. Kiss. Fight. Make love. Crazy like hell, young people today. Not like me when I was young." And still shaking his head and chuckling, he returned to his seat in a far corner of the café, clearly a regular customer and a solitary drinker, happy with his beer of glass in front of him, as he sat and surveyed the world outside. He ordered another beer, invited them to join him, smiled with understanding when they politely declined and was ready to survey them, as soon as they sat down at their table.

Jeremy's hands moved across the table, to reach for hers and enclose them warmly, fully. How she loved the totality of the surrender! Jeremy said, "Let me show you something," released her hands, and began to pull things out of his pocket. He pulled them out, one by one, and ranged them on the table beside the bottle of brandy, private exhibits of a secret longing, now no longer secret but allowed to be openly celebrated.

She stared at them. The sheer incongruity between their physical banality and the enormous emotional significance he had invested them with, struck her and she wanted to laugh out loud – the note she had written so many years ago, with its thin, cheap, copybook paper threatening to tear where it had been folded, the lipstick that he had borrowed from the café waitress, again some cheap brand with no name, the thin circlet of red thread that the fortune-teller in Change Koo Street had put round his wrist, after putting similar one round hers. She thought, "Oh my god, whatever happened to mine?"

This man had kept all these small tokens of remembrance all these years, as if they were priceless treasures. She suddenly realised she had no such tokens from him, not a letter, a postcard, a flower impulsively plucked from a bunch in a vase or a plant by the roadside, that she would have kept pressed between the pages of a book, or in a secret compartment in a purse. They too would have love's consecrating power.

Jeremy said, "I had told you, in my last visit, that it was your letter that had kept my hopes and dreams alive all this while. I did not mention the other links to you, just as dear." He told her that Florence had one day discovered the lipstick and kicked up a row. The lipstick mark on the collar was the proverbial give-away; a whole lipstick called for an explanation. Florence listened to his story. She said she wanted the full account. Then, unable to accuse him of infidelity, she berated him for the folly of fantasy.

Jeremy said to Li-ann, "Those days were horrible. Florence kept saying she could deal with infidelity, but not fidelity to a dream from which she was excluded."

Li-ann recalled the precise words, at that recent meeting at the airport, when Florence had said angrily, "It would have been better for him to tell me straight to my face, 'I don't love you anymore,' and go out and have an affair. I could cope with that better." In Florence's neat, precise world, dreams with their messiness had no place.

Jeremy put the items of remembrance back into his pocket and said, with a smile, "You women think you have a monopoly of sentiment. If I tell you how much this insignificant piece of thread has meant to me..." He held up the item for special attention before finally putting it away.

She remembered clearly the old fortune-teller in the ridiculous robe and cap, fastening upon them a rich promise of love in abundance and perpetuity.

"You will always be bound to each other," he had intoned. The old man realised that love needed to be pulled out of its abstract state and invested with a visibility, whether of good luck red thread o solid commitment.

When would Jeremy make that commitment? She had lived long enough in the real world to know that, in the end, a dream was of little value unless it came down upon solid ground and clothed itself with the colours and smells and textures of life's earthbound realities. *I love you. Marry me. Name the engagement day. Name the wedding day.* Kim, Suneetha, Jennie and the rest would have insisted on commitment's verbalisation, wedding date, the formal seeking of parental blessing. For her, an unequivocal, unqualified declaration, for which the kiss in the Rasa Sayang Hotel was surely a prelude, would be enough.

How happy she was, waiting got the words to shape on his lips! But still the man would delay the supreme moment, relishing the deliciousness of the present because for the first time he was able to talk freely about the past.

Seventeen

Jeremy said, "I'd told you about that long walk by myself in the woods, when the moment of truth came to me, when a new world seemed to break suddenly upon me, and I saw. I saw things clearly for the first time. It was a blinding clarity, after which things were never the same again. I hadn't told you then, but I'll tell you now, I saw you clearly as you were on that evening of 29 February 1980, at the airport when you said to me, 'I loved you so much. So much and so foolishly,' before turning round and running away. That image haunted me, but I suppressed it, as something I couldn't cope with. I beat it back ruthlessly, and thought I had succeeded in getting rid of it completely and putting my life on course again. Of course I was wrong. Florence saw everything. She has an uncanny instinct for smelling out the truth. She didn't like it, and asked for a separation. Indeed, that very day, she packed her bags and left to stay in a hotel."

The man could not stop talking. It was as if the heart had to be cleared of its load of confusions from the past, to make way for the certainties of the present. He said, "When Florence told me she wanted to divorce me, I took a walk in the woods again, and this time surrendered myself totally to the dear image. I wanted to keep it whole and entire, except for a small change. You had said, 'I loved you so much.' I wanted the past tense changed to the present: 'I love you so much.'"

It was an eerie sensation that filled her whole body with a mix of joy and disappointment. Those precious words – they were her utterance. Why was he not uttering his own, instead of quoting hers? Then she felt tears coming into her eyes. She was loved by a good man, and he was allowing his feelings for her, so long suppressed, to bubble up to the surface, like a pure, sparkling spring.

Jeremy said, "People fantasize and see what is not there. I'll tell you what my problem was. Reverse hallucination. Not seeing what was there. You were there all the time, but I didn't see."

Now she was openly crying. Jeremy leaned across, picked up her hand and kissed it tenderly. The elderly man sitting in a corner, drinking his beer and watching all this while, called out cheerfully, "Good for you! Good for you!" understanding that tears expressed joy better than anything else.

Jeremy said, "I love you," and her overcharged heart allowed no reciprocation in words nor gesture; she merely looked down and wiped her tears. Their keen observer from his corner, enjoying his role as love's cheerleader, held up a cocked thumb to indicate love's final victory, and called out once more, "Good for you! Good for you!"

He must have been the first to see or hear the first signs of trouble, for she saw him starting up from the table with an expression of alarm, before she noticed, to her utter astonishment, an angry young woman standing in front of them, but turned fully to face Jeremy, accusatory arms waving about wildly in the air.

"How can you..." she was gasping, both from anger and tiredness, for it was clear she had walked a long distance. "You said you would be back at the hotel – Dylan was almost crying for you – I had so much difficulty getting a taxi – and then that stupid taxi-driver couldn't find the Blue Paradise Café and went round and round, until I stopped him..."

Jeremy had started up in the utmost alarm, knocking his chair over. "I said I would be back," he said defensively. "I said I would be back before ten o'clock..."

"You know what the time it is now?" shrieked the woman. And poor Dylan crying and hungry and not yet taken his medicine..." It was at this point that Li-ann noticed a small, pale, sad-looking boy standing near her, looking at everybody with large, wounded eyes.

"Dylan!" Jeremy rushed towards him and held him tightly in his arms.

"Dylan, are you all right? Daddy's sorry. Really sorry. I shouldn't have..." He pressed his son against him, full of contrition. Then he looked up, as if he had forgotten something, and hastened to do a quick introduction. "Li-ann, this is Francine, Dylan's teacher. And this is my son, Dylan."

The man, in the midst of a threatening crisis, was actually trying to get his shy son to say "hello" and shake her hand. Francine was not even looking at her, being resolutely turned towards Jeremy all this while. She started to berate him all over again.

"Jeremy, how could you do such a thing to me and Dylan? And us not sure whether we should wait for you to come back or order dinner first. In the end, we had to come looking for you. Good thing the rain had stopped. Good thing I remembered the name of the café you mentioned. Jeremy, how could you..."

The prolonged remonstrances, those of a wife or fiancée or partner entitled to the language of marital reproach of a husband's remissness, were clearly for her benefit. She had invested Florence's name with much cold beauty in her imagination; she had not thought enough of the son's scheming teacher to paint a mental portrait. Perhaps that was because Florence had disdained to mention the rival by name.

Francine was neither beautiful nor plain. Unlike Florence, she would never stand out in a crowd. Like Florence, she had a shrewd instinct for smelling out the truth, which she was now all out to deny and to destroy.

She turned from angry accusation of the father to solicitous affection for the son. "My poor little Dylan," she said, drawing him to herself, putting her arms around him and pressing her lips upon the top of his head. "You're okay, my sweetheart. Francine will take care of you."

Li-Ann remembered Florence's advice. Get him. Work on the son. The best way is through his son, whom he'll die for. Florence, in trying to pit her against the hated Francine, was recommending the enemy's strategy.

Francine, with Dylan pressed to her side, turned to face Li-Ann for the first time, and said curtly, "We have to get back to the hotel. It's late. We're all hungry and tired." Then she turned to Jeremy and still assuming the authoritative tone of domestic familiarity said, "Get a taxi."

We. We. Our hotel. Clearly, this woman meant to say to her, as to an interloper: Stay out. Jeremy, I and Dylan, we are together as a family, in the intimacy of a hotel, on vacation together. No matter what he may tell, we are, the three of us, already a family. So stay out.

Li-Ann would always marvel at the calmness with which she

turned to Jeremy and ask, "Would you please tell me what is going on."

His face was the face of a man totally nonplussed, overtaken by events over which he had no control. "Wait… please… let me…" He stretched out a hand to Li-ann. She refused to take it, still maintaining a calmness which she knew would not last. She continued to look fixedly at him. It only made things worse that he continued to stare at her and gasp incoherently, and that meanwhile, Francine had moved up, slipped her arm though his, and stood there, looking at her with cool contempt.

"Wait," cried Jeremy miserably. "Please wait. Let me explain."

The word burst in her ears like the deadliest of poisons. "Explanation?" she cried, and by this time, the calmness had left her. Shock and rage constricted her throat and made her words come out as small, strangled sounds. "Explanation? You've come to Singapore with someone else, and all the time you made me believe…" She could not go on.

"Wait, please listen. It's not as you think."

It's not as you think. He was resorting to the cheap language of a man's protestations of innocence. "Don't bother to say anymore. Goodbye."

"Wait…" cried Jeremy, trying to stop her. "Li-ann, please…"

And it was at this point that a number of things happened, turning the scene into pure pandemonium. Dylan began to cry, Francine flung down a vase in a fit of temper and began to scream at Jeremy again, a small crowd gathered to watch, and the elderly man in the corner hurried over to see what he could do to help. He was beginning to reek strongly of beer. He went from one person to another in a melodrama of placation, saying earnestly, "Never mind. Never mind. These things happen. We forgive and forget. Kiss and make up. Love one another. Love is all that matters in the end." He slipped on something, fell to the floor, and lay there, still gesturing extravagantly "Never mind. Kiss and make up. You must love one another."

By now Li-ann was trembling so much she thought that she too would fall down in an ignominious heap on the floor. But she managed to shake off Jeremy's arm, to break free and run out of the café. Once out in the open, she took a deep breath of air and began running away as fast as she could, not having the least idea of where she was going.

She could hear Jeremy running after her. "Stop!" he yelled. "Please stop. Let me explain."

This man was born to be her torment and her joy. The joy was over. The torment would be greater with the explanation. Explanation. It would be the most hateful word to her from now onwards, because it would be the greatest betrayer of love's truth, the greatest tarnisher of its purity. For explanations always involved the desperation of lies and deceit.

Still running, she cast off, as she would throw off a cursed shadow, the last sounds of his call behind her, and without looking back once, knew that he had stopped running after her, and had turned and started walking back to Francine and Dylan, to get ready to take them back to their hotel.

It would dawn on her only after she had reached home, locked herself in her room and lain very still on her bed, that there was a fearful pattern to all the 29 February meetings. Each had begun with the sweetest hopes, the highest expectations; each had invariably ended crashing into an abyss of darkest, bitterest despair. From henceforth, the Leap Year would be that portion of Time's territory, small but deadly, that no woman with a loving heart should ever wander into. Every four years, for just twenty four hours, Fate, if it meant to be kind to mortals, should put up the sign: Danger. Keep out.

She found herself crying softly into her pillow, and was glad that this was one of those rare nights when her mother was not at home, allowing herself the treat of an overnight mahjong session in a friend's house.

She fell into a fitful sleep and had a dream in which she saw Jeremy and herself in some beautiful room in the Rasa Sayang Hotel, dancing to soft music. Jeremy was holding her in his arms and about to kiss her. "Wait a minute," she said sternly to him. "What about that explanation. I want to hear your explanation."

He said, "I love my wife because I married her. I love Francine because she is crazy about my son and is good for him. I love you because you love me so much. A man can love different women for different reasons, can't he?"

Somebody echoed cheerfully, "Can't he?" and she saw Danny Sim, Kim's faithless husband standing by Jeremy's side and grinning broadly. Danny said, "You women, you want to be first and last in a man's affections. You are *so-ooo* unrealistic!" Now it was Jeremy's turn to echo, and he said, raising his voice to a bellow, "You are *so-ooo* unrealistic! Welcome to the real world!"

In a rage, she began hitting his chest-with her fists and crying, "Stop it, Jeremy! Don't you see how you're upsetting me?" And then she was so upset that she drove him out of the hotel into the road, into pouring rain. She seemed to be in some enclosed space, with a locked door, and he was outside the door, begging to come in. "Please, Li-ann, let me in."

His voice grew insistent, in the roaring rain. She woke with a start, and heard the sound of wind and rain outside her window, as if it had broken out of the dream and got mixed with the reality. The voice too, seemed to have done exactly that, penetrating her consciousness and tugging at her eyelids to force them to open. "Li-ann," it pleaded, "please let me in."

It was only after she sat up, aware of a violent headache, that she realised that the voice was real, coming from outside the main door. She heard the words distinctly, "Li-ann, you have to allow me to explain." Something inside her screamed: "This man's love is the toxic legacy of a dream gone so wrong. Flee him, at all costs," and she slid down under the sheets, and covered her face and ears tightly with her pillows. "Please go away," she whispered into the darkness, "I cannot bear any more of the pain."

She heard the sound of a window shutter opening and closing; a suspicious neighbour must have peered into the darkness, seen a shadow at her door, and was trying to frighten off the intruder. She listened to the sound of footsteps fading away in the night's silence, and said once more to herself, "I cannot bear any more of the pain."

Eighteen

In 1989, Li-ann wrote a book of short stories, which was published by a leading local publishing house. To her delight, it was very well received by the public. One of the reviewers even described her as "one of Singapore's most promising young writers, certainly one to watch."

The title of the book, *Of the Heart, From the Heart*, was misleading, as was the cover, showing that organ, tender and palpitating, beside a red rose on a stalk, denuded of all its petals which lay in a heap nearby, like so many drops of blood. Kim, Suneetha, Jennie and the others in The Group, who did not know about the book until they received the invitation cards for its launch at a tea reception hosted by the publishing house, got together to speculate about the significance of the double reference to 'heart' in the title.

"Do you think she's unburdening the secrets of her own heart?"

"She doesn't tell us much, though we're her close friends, so she's doing it through a book."

"It was terrible, from what I gather. I mean, their last meeting. She was devastated. That man's a beast!"

"Last meeting? Do you think he'll come again on 29 February

1992?"

"He'd better not. I have the impression she's successfully worked him out of her system."

"What a strange tale. Pursuit of the impossible dream, embodied in a weird man living thousands of miles away, who comes only every Leap Year."

"Came. Past tense. Li-ann will never see him again. The dream's over."

"Li-ann will tell you that dreams are never over. She's so strange! But then again, after her terrible experience…"

"*Of the Heart, From the Heart*. To think that we'll get to understand the heart of a close friend only indirectly through her fiction."

"Li-ann's such a private person I bet she reveals nothing in those stories. I can't wait!"

The friends, intent on scrutinising every tale in the book to pull out hidden meanings, were very disappointed to find that the stories were not love stories at all but simple portrayals of everyday people, including an old woman who picked up rotting or damaged vegetables discarded by stall-holders in the market, cut and cleaned them and sold them in little piles for a few cents each; a prosperous businessman who yearned for a male child after a succession of female children; a temple medium who had strange dreams of the gods and went into the most shocking trances; a teacher whose sole passion in life was getting her students to score top grades in her subject in a national examination; a young student whose compositions for her English language teacher were always full of appalling grammar mistakes but also of astute observations of life remarkable of one so young.

Li-ann, who had always wanted to write a book, would

never have believed that the motivation, in the end, would be sheer desperation. For she was desperate to forget, to fill up the present with activity, so that, like a river in abundant flood, it would spill over, backwards, into the past to cover up unhappy memories and, forwards, into the future, to block out unwelcome thoughts.

She had tried to distract herself with a frenzied programme that required both physical and mental exertion, including a gruelling camping trip in the wilds of Malaysia, and a mammoth fund-raising project for a group of charities, for which she tramped the streets of Singapore in the hot sun, carrying a donation box.

But the most effective activity for forgetting, was writing a book. For it was not only the planning and writing out of the eighteen short stories, but a whole set of activities calculated to consume a huge amount of energy, time and attention. She had numerous discussions with editors, made endless phone calls to consult about this or check on that, did meticulous proof-reading and finally helped in the preparations for the launch, for which she was required to make an appropriate speech. She zipped through each activity with great enthusiasm, and after the launch, did her own evaluation of how successful she had been in her self-initiated programme of the heart's healing. The verdict was: Excellent.

K.S. took her out for dinner to celebrate the book. Still aware but not too perturbed by the hostility of his wife towards his best friend, he had decided on a simple solution to keep both women happy: make clear to each the precise nature of his relationship with the other, then put them on separate tracks, parallel to each other but never meeting. Thus he had told Jocelyn, "I love you very much, but that doesn't mean I can't occasionally see

Li-ann whom I've known and loved for a long time."

It had been a daring and clever move, to establish, in one utterance, once and for all, the two kinds of love that can co-exist in a married man's life without him needing to feel guilty. Jocelyn had pondered the words carefully, and come to the conclusion that, one, her husband would never cheat on her; two, being the stubborn, independent-minded man that he was, he would be the more inclined to cheat, the more she opposed him and, three, Li-ann was not the type of woman to steal other people['s husbands.

So K.S., married man and soon-to-be father, was able to have a dinner date with Li-ann, needing to fear no more than a sarcastic comment or two from his wife, when he got home.

Li-ann said, "'Kit Sing'. How strange I didn't know what your initials stood for, until so many years later. But you'll always be 'K.S.' to me. My god, how long have we known each other?" It was an appropriate time for them both, he contentedly settled in marriage and domestic comfort and she enjoying a rare period of peace in mind and heart, for gentle reminiscence.

"Since Secondary Three. Remember our first day in Class 3C in Lum Kah Secondary? I threw a paper dart at you, and you pretended not to notice. I threw three more, and then you hurled all back, a whole fistful."

"I remember. You were disgusting. Loud. Uncouth. Untidy. Boastful."

"And you were snobbish and pert and high-and-mighty. Speaking perfect English. Sniggering at poor Mr Teh, the maths teacher who couldn't speak one grammatically correct sentence to save his life. You were heartless."

"You were a nuisance. Never doing your homework. Peeking into my book, to copy my work."

"You were self-centred and selfish. Hoarding information. Not sharing it with others, as all good Singaporeans should."

They laughed together, as in the old days. The laughter could only be for the years in school; it could not be for the university years when the schoolboy warmth had suddenly flared into a consuming passion, that for so long refused to give up hope, and gave so much pain. K.S.'s love for her had provided much matter for talk in the university campus.

Would they dare talk about that dreadful evening at the Blue Paradise Café, when he had stormed out in bitter rage, and she had been contrite ever since?

K.S. said, "It's wonderful, isn't it, being able to talk like this. But there's something we've been avoiding. As long as it remains lurking in the background, a dark detritus at the bottom of memory's jar, it will be the annoying pebble in the shoe. Forgive my horribly mixed metaphors, but you know what I'm referring to."

He needed to tell her about the anger and pain she had caused; she needed to tell him how very sorry she was. It was amazing how the most difficult things to say or do are rendered easy by the simple passage of time.

They reached across the table to touch each other's hands, immensely relieved and happy. In the end, the ghosts of the past, like the genie in a bottle cast into the sea, cannot be fully exorcised, until one hauls up the bottle from the watery depths, uncorks it, pulls the genie out of the darkness of both bottle and sea, and pushes it into bright sunlight, where it instantly loses all power to frighten and subdue.

The last remaining ghost in their shared memory was gone forever. From now onwards, they could talk about anything freely, and even joke about it. They had taken their friendship to the highest level of trust.

K.S. said, "I love you, Li-ann," and she replied, "I love you too," both secure in the innocence of that other meaning of this portentous word. K.S. would always be her best and dearest friend. She would see him through his many reverses of fortune in the 90s, when he lost a lot of money in a foolish business importing scuba-diving equipment, when his wife gave birth to a daughter with Down's Syndrome and everything seemed to be falling apart. But this was 1989 when K.S. was truly happy and contented, and had put on weight, so that in both appearance and temperament, he was different from the intense, sardonic, skinny young man of the undergraduate years.

K.S. said, slowly and thoughtfully, holding in his hand a copy of the book she had just autographed for him, "There's something I want to ask you. But don't answer if you don't want to."

"I thought we had reached that stage when we could ask each other anything," said Li-ann cheerfully. She saw K.S. looking at the page after the title page, where she had made a dedication, and she knew what he was going to say next.

"Li-ann, you've dedicated this book to 'J'. Pardon me for being nosy, but I thought the writing of the book was precisely to forget him. Don't mind my asking, Li-ann. Just a nosy old friend wanting to know."

"Not at all," said Li-ann brightly. "Read the inscription under the name."

K.S. read: "'Without whom this book would never have been written.'" The most mundane of inscriptions, once inspired and inspiring, now hackneyed and stale, meant to pay the warmest tribute to spouse, friend or colleague, for having made so many sacrifices for the sake of the book.

Li-ann said, "You can see I'm using the words in an ironic, twisted way. Without the need to forget the pain caused by Jeremy, I would never have written the book, something I'd always wanted to do, as you know. A kind of reverse inspiration, if you like." It was the first time in a long while that she had mentioned him by name. Her eyes shone with the brightness of a new and defiant strength.

K.S. picked up her hand to press against his lips, murmuring, "Dear, dear Li-ann," and was not quite sure what else to say. "You know, K.S., I couldn't have told anyone but you," said Li-ann warmly, "because you've always understood me best even when you've disagreed with me most. K.S., I needed to expel the last ghost from the bottle! And I needed to confront it squarely, right in the face, and say, 'There! I'm not running away from you anymore!'"

The idea had suddenly come to her when the book was already about to go to press. She called her publisher and breathlessly asked, 'I still in time to put in a dedication?' The publisher, expecting a warm tribute to the mother, saw the single letter 'J', tantalising, teasing, unmatched with the mundaneness of the standard "without whom", but was too tactful to ask.

At the launch, everyone agreed that Li-ann never looked prettier nor happier. Her friends as usual came together for speculative, whispered sharing.

"Do you think she's got over him?"

"Doesn't appear to be so. A dedication is a very personal, serious thing."

"Don't know about Li-ann. She's full of surprises."

"Do you think he'll come again for 29 February 1992?"

"He shouldn't. Not when she's got back on her feet again. She should have learnt her lesson."

"But she's dedicated the book to him! Clearly, she means to convey some message indirectly to him."

"He'll never get to know about it. This is only a locally published book. It is unlikely to be sold in Canada."

"'J' could stand for so many names. I think her mother has a Western name, 'Janet' or 'Janice'. And that K.S. who was so crazy about her until he got married. He may have another name – John, Joseph, James, Jeffrey – or a nickname. They are still very close."

K.S., who called to give Li-ann a video she wanted, asked, "Is it working?"

"Is what working?"

"The dedication. The confronting of the last ghost in the bottle."

"Yes. It will never bother me again."

Nineteen

The letters from Vancouver had started arriving in 1989, and by 1990, had grown into a large stack, which she kept, unopened, in a box in a drawer, tied with a piece of ribbon. By 1991, they had filled the box and spilled into the empty space in the drawer, still unopened.

The first letter had been the real test. She was reading the newspaper and her mother, in another part of the room, was going through the day's mail. She heard a little gasp of surprise, and saw her mother pick up a white envelope to stare at its postmark. "Here, it's for you."

Now it was her turn to show surprise. She jumped up from the sofa and snatched the letter with indecent eagerness. Then she took it to her room, closing the door.

Mrs Chang thought, *this is not a good sign. She hasn't got over him.* Her daughter's Dream Man had become the Detestable Monster of horror movies who had come charging into their lives, wreaking havoc. He was now only a memory; if only he would be an irrelevance as well, with no power to return, to continue the damage.

Mrs Chang's greatest regret in the whole sorry business which she would never understand as long as she lived, was that the man, a total stranger, had stolen so many years of her daughter's life and made it a dereliction, when it should have been radiant with success and happiness. Her one consolation was that he had left at a time when Li-ann was still young enough and attractive enough to go out and meet other men. If only she would! Mrs Chang, thinking over the matter in the quiet of her room, always ended with much sad sighing and shaking of the head. So much beauty and talent, all gone to waste, when they could have secured the most eligible bachelor in Singapore. If only. Mrs Chang was resigned to thinking of her daughter's future in the language of futile hope.

Li-ann would be thirty three soon – horror of horrors! – and still, there was no man in the horizon to provide any degree of solace. Thirty, thirty five, forty, fifty. The image was frightening, of herself and Li-ann, both old and grey, both pinched and soured, each providing no consolation to the other as they walked together down the long bleak corridor of years. Mrs Chang thought of other mothers in the same sad situation, and took comfort in a growing sorority of mothers in Singapore linked by the common sorrow of having unmarried daughters on their hands.

She passed Li-ann's room and paused to listen. Small sounds were coming from inside, but not of an envelope being torn open, or sheets of letter-paper held in the hands. Mrs Chang once more shook her head, sighed and walked on.

Li-ann, sitting on her bed, looked at the letter by her side. To open or not to open. The decision was crucial; its outcome could very well undo the work of months spent in the reclaiming of peace of mind, in the re-establishing of some semblance of order in a woefully disordered life.

What could he possibly have to tell her that would be of any good to her now?

Let me explain. She had long ago decided that no explanation could ever justify the unconscionable act of coming to declare his love for her, while being holed up with another in a hotel room. The presence of the son might be brought up as a mitigating factor, but the appalling, unpardonable fact remained: he was with another woman.

You may like to know that I am now married and very happy. His letter could be one of pure information about his new life, reeking of marital bliss, and ending with the hope that she would still be his friend. Never, never. She thought, "I will never be a puppet on your string again, one moment a lover, another a friend, yet another a soulmate, always dancing to the tune of your selfish needs."

I love you. The declaration that had been so sweet to her ears, so joyous to a heart in long and patient waiting, had become a ringing falsehood, and would acquire the additional opprobrium of an insult if made once more in writing. No, no. The man who lived in his own world with its own rules, ignorant or careless about other people's deserved no attention. Anything remotely connected with him should be instantly destroyed.

She struck a match, and picked up the letter to put it to the small hissing flame, to consign it to oblivion forever. Every single letter that might follow would meet a similar fate. That man would not be allowed into her life anymore, whether in his actual presence or by the proxy of letters, postcards, photographs, whatever he might send.

But she blew out the flame, and rubbed out the burnt part of the envelope. The letter inside was intact.

"No," she thought fiercely. "I mustn't run away." The ghost in the dark bottle or closet: she would face it boldly, and expose it to the light that it feared. She would read the letter and allow whatever feelings it elicited to express themselves freely and fully, then laugh in its face and say, "There. I'm not afraid."

She began to tear the envelope, her fingers trembling. She stopped, and once more let the letter drop to her side on the bed. There it lay, facing her. No, she couldn't read his letter, knowing what it was all about. It would reopen the old wounds and rob them of their last chance to heal. Yes, she would have the strength and confidence to read even the most outrageous lies desperately disguised as truth, as well as the pride and magnanimity to rise above the pettiness of jealousy and hurt, and send him a card that would say blithely "Congratulations on your marriage."

Yes, she would, could, should. No, she wouldn't, couldn't, shouldn't.

The dreaded headache was coming back with the wild swings of indecision. She was exhausted, and fell back on the bed closing her eyes and laying an arm across them. Finally she got up, opened a drawer and put the letter inside.

She knew she had made the right decision. For the mistake of opening this first letter could unleash a whole chain of uncontrollable events, like a massive swarm of insects released into the air and impossible to summon back into the manageability of nest or cage or box.

The letter, lying in the drawer, soon gathered around itself the fearful aura of ancient superstition: touch me, it said, and chaos will break out upon your world.

Over the months, as other letters followed, always in their white envelopes, always with her name and address written in a firm, clear hand, she was pleasantly surprised to discover that opening the drawer, dropping them inside and then going on with life as usual, was not such a difficult thing after all.

By the middle of 1991, when the letters required another box to hold them, she had grown accustomed to their presence, mysterious and yet not so, ominous and yet affording the secret pleasure of the conclusion that whatever his feelings for her had been or were, they were strong enough to persist in an exercise that could only bring him frustration and pain. She could see him writing each letter, folding it up, putting it in the white envelope, sealing the envelope, putting a stamp on it, dropping it in the mailbox, and then begin the tortuous wait for a reply he knew would not come.

His programme of self-punishment balanced hers of self-healing.

Without opening any of the letters, she knew the story they told, which was certainly gratifying to her, of a man who, in the strange upheavals of his life, had one point of stability – his determination to keep in touch with her. It was a lunatic, one-way communication, but he was persisting in it.

Would he come to see her on 29 February 1992 which was fast approaching?

By now, in the huge volume of writing that had gone into the continuous stream of letters over the years, he would have spoken of or hinted about his intention; indeed, she was almost certain all the letters were a prelude to the fulfilment, once again, of a vow that had taken hold of him in some strange way. But no! nothing would induce her to break her own vow of proud rejection of the letters, ultimate test of the will to free herself of him.

It was part of this stern pride that she checked her imagination as soon as it strayed, and pulled it back from the many images of the past that it had alighted on, like an erratically moving flashlight lighting up random objects in the darkness. The images were not only of themselves, but, unaccountably of people they had met in the briefest of brief encounters – the couple on the motorcycle, who had quarrelled; the old man who wanted the bottle of brandy; somebody at the wedding party, a thin man with a red carnation in his lapel, who offered them drinks; Kai Ma's caregiver (whose name she couldn't remember) in a blue blouse of floral print and grey trousers, the small Indian boy who had delivered her note. In her dreams, they moved about easily, melting in and out of one another, doing silly things that were silly even for dreams. Lest you forget, her dreams seemed to be saying and spitefully filled themselves with people she would be forced to connect with him.

She looked at the growing pile of letters and marvelled at her successful resolution, over the years, to defy their challenge to be read. Curiosity had ever been a powerful drive, but it had no power over resolute pride. She was beginning to feel a sense of control, very satisfying indeed, as one by one, his letters cried out to be opened and read, and she replied each time, "No, it is my wish that yours is denied." If she were to evaluate her performance now, it would rate an Excellent Plus.

29 February 1992. Let it come and go, like any other day in the year. She had long ago shaken from her feet the dust of the Blue Paradise Café, the Singapore associated with him had been erased from the map of her new resoluteness.

Neither place nor face could be so easily erased from the map of the unruly terrain of dreams at night. They were a mix of happy and unhappy dreams, the happy ones centring on a kiss, a touch, a clasp of hand, the unhappy ones on the kiss or touch transferred to another, a scheming woman who schemed even more shockingly in the dreams than in reality. In one, she saw Francine, lying on a hotel bed in a negligee, propped up on one elbow, with Dylan lying beside her. Jeremy was standing at the door, facing them. She said, "Jeremy, come get your son," and laughed as Jeremy bounded up, threw himself on the bed in laughing joy, and embraced them both. All three came together in a boisterously happy, tumbling heap.

Then she saw herself appearing in the room and going to stand by the bed to watch. "See what a happy family we are!" cried Francine, poking her head out of a mess of happily interlocked limbs to look at her and mock her. She saw a strap slip off Francine's shoulder, exposing a round, fair breast, and saw Jeremy upon her in an instant. "See what a great lover he is!" cried Francine again.

She hated her dreams at night. They seemed to have a life of their own and a special, mocking malice, to sour the waking hours. Soon even these dreams would be controlled and emptied of their poisonous content.

One afternoon towards the end of 1991, Li-ann came home and gave a shriek of alarm. The Filipino maid who came to do general housecleaning every week, and was on her way to the rubbish chute with a large plastic bag of something in her hand, stopped abruptly. Li-ann rushed to snatch the bag from her. A few of the unread letters fell out; she picked them up quickly.

"Maria," she cried, her face bearing the taut pallor of someone who has nearly lost a prized possession, "what on earth are you doing? Why are you throwing away these letters?"

The girl said, "Mam, they were lying all over the floor – I thought you didn't want them –"

"Didn't want them!" exploded Li-ann. "How can you say that? And they weren't all over the floor, Maria. They were neatly tied up in bundles." She had that morning cleaned the drawer, sprayed it with insecticide and left it to be aired, having earlier spotted a cockroach. Cockroaches could, over time, reduce the pile of unopened letters to shreds.

"They were unopened, Mam, so I thought you didn't want them anymore."

The girl's logic was infuriating. "Next time, Maria," said Li-ann severely, "don't touch any of my things."

Twenty

Towards the end of 1991, Li-ann told the group, "I'm ready." They squealed in delight and gave each other knowing looks. For she meant, "I'm ready to date again, so introduce me to all those interesting men you've been dangling before me for so long." Being happily married, they were, by virtue of that fact alone, duty bound to help their less fortunate sisters. For too long, Li-ann, easily the most attractive among their still single friends, had been, annoyingly, the least interested.

Kim, Suneetha, and Jennie had husbands who had friends or business associates who formed a very convenient and desirable pool of marital potential upon which the women, flushed with the glow of magnanimous influence, could concentrate their efforts as matchmakers. The self-given role had its special gratifications, not least of which was the impunity with which a married woman could surround herself with attractive men and flirt with them right under her husband's nose. Kim, Suneetha and Jennie, between them, came up with an impressive array of highly eligible men, known collectively as The Catch, whom they painted, for Li-ann's benefit, in the brightest colours of husbandly worthiness. They must have, in the course of their numerous lunches and high teas which had become a regular ritual of sorority over the years, brought up the names of a hundred such worthies.

When the actual work of matchmaking began, the number was realistically cut down to four. Thus identified, the four men were arranged in order of general attractiveness. They were, in that order, a banker named Wu Tai Sun who had the best wine-cellar in the whole of Singapore; a lawyer named Eric George who had the most charming manners, a businessman whom everyone called 'Captain', and who owned the popular Dallas Supremo Pub, and an academic named Daniel Tse who did not have the wealth of any of the others but held a highly respected position in the university.

They were all thus lined up for Li-ann's inspection and choice. She could systematically go down the list, and date each in turn, giving herself any amount of time to ponder, pick and choose. Or, if she wanted to save time, she could date all of them at the same time, apportioning to each a fair and equal share of the time in her calendar.

Li-ann said, "You are assuming, my dear girls, that all these gorgeous men are at my beck and call? I'm already thirty three, you know. Way past prime time, as my mum would say."

Kim said, giving her a sly wink: "That banker Wu Tai Sun has been pestering me for months for an introduction. He said he saw us at lunch at The Meridien once, but was too shy to come up to say hello."

Jennie said, "Thirty three too old? A woman is at her best then. Let me tell you this: the charming lawyer Erie George tells me he is not interested in women younger than thirty. He finds them silly and immature. You are his kind of woman."

The markers for the highly interesting game thus established, Li-ann said, "Well, what are you waiting for?" and set Kim the immediate task of arranging for the first introduction.

In the end, the noble enterprise collapsed into a fiasco.

Li-ann had put aside a month in her calendar for the entire process of meeting, scrutinising, eliminating and final choice. But after two weeks, she whispered urgently to her friends, "Help. Get me out."

"What on earth's the matter with you?" demanded Kim. "Didn't you find anyone interesting enough?"

"I'm sorry," said Li-ann. "I think I yawned too much on one date." It had been much worse than that. She had actually fallen asleep halfway through the banker's long recitation of his stock holdings, during dessert, until something dropped from the table and woke her up.

"Didn't Captain charm you? He can be so gallant." But the truth was that Li-ann was unable to remember Captain and her dinner date with him; she vaguely recollected a florid face wreathed in smiles and a bright purple silk shirt.

"You're too picky as always!"

Her mother would have come up with the same accusation, if she had known. She had been watching Li-ann get ready for each date with intense interest, and peeping out of the window to catch a glimpse of each gentleman before he drove off. But Li-ann assiduously evaded all her questions, fearing to be accused, once again, of letting the big fish get away.

Kim said severely, "Li-ann, you're making all our efforts go to waste.'"

"Girls, I can't marry someone who wears a massive jade ring and says he enjoys Shakespeare's Lomeo and Julia very much!"

"Li-ann, for your sake we'll send him for a course in grooming or correct pronunciation at the British Council."

They all laughed loudly together, the nature of the

matchmaking game being one that afforded as much merriment in its failure as in its success.

To placate her friends, Li-ann decided to give the last gentleman on the list, Professor Daniel Tse, another chance. He was the one she liked best. She went out on several dinner dates with him, and each time, gave enough encouragement for him to call the next morning, to arrange for the next date. The professor was by no means handsome or sparkling, but he had a strong, pleasant-looking face and a rich, deep voice very suited to his discussion of this or that scientific or philosophical theory, which interested her very much.

The professor tried to hold her hand on the second date, and to kiss her on the fourth. But she always moved away adroitly. In the end he gave up.

He said, suddenly looking at her critically and saying with brutal honesty, since he knew they would never go out together again, "There's something the matter with you, which I cannot pinpoint. But I think it's got to do with this thing called emotional baggage from the past. You've never spoken about it, but it's there all the time, colouring your every thought and action. I think you have a problem." Unrequited interest could turn nasty; the professor's tone became increasingly smoother, as his criticism grew sharper, until he was telling her, in almost silken tones, that he thought she needed professional help.

Li-ann winced to the man's severe lashing. She merely said, "Oh, I had no idea it was that bad!" and was glad the evening was over.

In January 1992, she noticed that there were fewer letters. It was an odd situation in which, knowing nothing of their contents, she knew everything about their dates of arrival, their dates of departure from Vancouver, their size and relative weight, as if she could tell that one contained only a single sheet of paper and another at least five, the slight changes in his transcription of her name and address on the envelope face, sometimes writing out her name in full, sometimes only her initials. She could even differentiate the letters by urgency of tone, sensing one letter to be more serious or insistent or pleading than another.

People read letters, then threw them away. She never read hers, but kept them. It was an odd situation, to say the least, but she was beginning to enjoy a certain sense of confidence, almost of power, as she dropped each letter into the drawer, straight from the mailbox. Sometimes she opened the drawer to have a look at them, and wondered if the writer knew they went unread. What manner of person could keep writing over such a long period of time, without having received a single reply?

One day in early February 1992, she held the most recently arrived letter in her hand and slowly turned it about in her hand, as she made her way towards the drawer. She sensed the urgency of a message through the envelope, and stood undecided for a long time before the open drawer. Then tremblingly, she picked up a paper cutter and slit open the envelope. As she pulled out the letter which was only one sheet of paper, she felt the strange unease of one breaking a sacred resolution or taboo for the first time.

She was reading, for the first time, a letter which could be his last, in a long line of hundreds, that stretched back to 1989. It was a one-line letter and it said, "Please let me see you on 29 February 1992."

No, no, she thought. You must never see me again. You must never write to me again. I have been playing a dangerous game for too long. You are bad news, Jeremy Matthew Lee Yu-min.

Now she understood the frisson that had run through her body when she held the letter. It was the only one that needed a response. She wrote back immediately. It was also a one-sentence letter: "Please don't come to see me, not 29 February 1992, not ever."

Back came his reply on a postcard which, because of its openness, could be read even against one's will. It said, "Li-ann, please let me. I love you."

She put her hands up to her ears, as if the words had been shouted at her in a deafening roar, once again a ringing mockery. For he had said them, while committed to another woman, holed up with her in a hotel, on happy vacation. And he was saying them now, probably from his position as happily married man in need of diversion. He must have meant her to understand them in all their implied qualifications: I love you, but there is also the love for Francine. I love you, but I can't ever love you – do you know what I mean?

This man had distorted and twisted a word that ought to be sacrosanct, treating it like putty in his hands, to fit into the shape of his every need. There it was all again – the unquestionably well-meaning but spoilt and selfish man who must have his cake and eat it. If she went to meet him once more in the Blue Paradise Café, would she see yet another woman with him, whom he would calmly introduce? He would love a whole line of women through the years, with his expansive, indiscriminating heart. She would never condescend to be in that line, but the greater humiliation was that he never even considered her worthy of it. All he wanted was for her to be on the outside, for him to turn to for consolation and strength. He had assigned her that role.

Intolerable! Intolerable!

In the midst of her vexation, one gratifying feeling stood out:

through the wild changes and fluxes in this man's life: she was the only constant. But she could dispense with that gratification.

She had an idea. She would write him a letter that would be more than a curt one-liner. She did a draft of her letter, to make sure her words were clear, precise and above all, dignified. She wrote: "Please don't feel obliged to keep a vow you made so long ago, probably very impulsively. We don't need to be enslaved by the tyranny of promises. Since only the beneficiary of a vow can free its originator of it, I say now: It doesn't exist anymore. You are free of it."

The reply came very soon: "I'll be waiting for you on the evening of 29 February, not in the Blue Paradise Café but in the Rasa Sayang Hotel which too has fond memories for me. When I see you – I know you will come – my first words will be 'Will you love me as I love you?' and your reply will be 'Yes' – I know it already."

The man was preposterous in his presumptions. How dare he! No, cried Li-ann. with a ferocity of both look and voice. If I go again, I will be subjecting myself to another of those humiliations you seem so adept in dishing out, Jeremy. It takes longer than four years, you know, to recover. So it's no, no and no again. You are bad news, Jeremy Matthew Lee Yu-min. You always have been.

She received a note, just two days before 29 February 1992. It said: "I'll be waiting for you at eight o'clock in the Rasa Sayang Hotel, in a restaurant on the first floor, called The Blue Heaven. Isn't that a wonderful coincidence?"

The man was impossible! He was bulldozing his selfish way through all opposition, showing not the least respect or. regard for her wishes. He had to be taught a lesson.

Twenty One

It was inconvenient that Kim had sent over Lynette on the afternoon of 29 February 1992, to spend the day with her. The girl had been naughty and unruly at home, bullying her little brother and sister and giving endless trouble to the maids. The adorable child had become a troubled little girl, given to fits of temper and long bouts of sullenness. It would only be years later that Kim and her husband Danny would acknowledge the effects of their marital conflicts on their daughter. They had assumed that with all the toys and gifts and pampering from the adults, she would be immune. But the child, bright and sensitive, proud and secretive, watched, listened, suffered and lashed out in the confusion and pain of her little heart. Only her godmother Li-ann could get her to behave.

Lynette said, watching Li-ann take out all the letters from the drawer and putting them in a large box, "What are you doing, Godma?" She had to repeat her question several times, yelling the last one in petulant impatience, before Li-ann snapped out of her thoughts.

"Godma, listen to me! You never listen anymore!"

Li-ann explained patiently that she was taking the letters to a friend. A child's questions could be so inconvenient. "What's his name?"

"Jeremy."

"Jeremy what?"

"Jeremy Matthew Lee Yu-min." She had assiduously avoided the mention of his name over the years, even to herself, so that its articulation, coming slowly out of her mouth, sounded very strange to her ears.

"Why are you taking these letters to him?"

There would be no end to the child's whys. Li-ann decided to cut through all of them, not with an answer but a stern order.

"Lynette, I want you to listen carefully to me. It's something very, very important. We're going to have our dinner early tonight, then I'm going out. It's for something very important, as I told you. I'll be back shortly. You don't have to tell Auntie Chang. If she asks, just say I've gone out and will be back shortly. Are you listening, Lynette?"

The little girl's eyes grew wide with the exciting prospect of being involved in some adult conspiracy.

"Yes, Godma."

"Good girl! Now will you leave Godma for a while, so that she can get ready."

"Godma," said Lynette, looking at her thoughtfully, "are you ill?"

"No, sweetheart. Why do you ask?"

"Godma, this Jeremy Matthew Lee Yu-min,"(the child had a fantastic memory even for difficult names), "is he a bad man?"

"I don't think so, Lynette."

Out of the mouths of babes.

In her car, on the way to the Rasa Sayang Hotel, her heart was at its most turbulent ever, thumping wildly, like a frenzied bird knocking madly against its cage. At one point, she had to stop, park her car by the side of a road and pause to calm herself. Beside her, on the passenger seat, was the box of letters, neatly tied with string.

Someone pressed a grinning face against the car window pane, and made her scream. It was only a drunk, and she waved him away angrily.

"Oh my god," she gasped, overcome by the enormity of the task before her. She decided that one way of calming herself was to practise, slowly and carefully, the little speech she had prepared for the occasion. She had written it down, then committed it to memory, to ensure that the high tension that would surely rule the occasion, would not make her say the wrong thing, come out with the wrong inflection. Everything had to be right, for this was going to be the last time that she would see him, their last 29 February meeting, after which a bizarre vow made so many years ago and carried out with such bizarre consequences over so many years, would be swallowed up in the resumption of ordinary life, to be lived through in quiet and untroubled simplicity.

But before that, she had to allow herself the full discharge of the heart's bitterness. Yes, she would do that! The heart needed its moment of victory, before it would submit to the quietude of forgiveness and forgetting. This was the closure she needed.

She rehearsed the entire scene in her head, as she drove slowly through the brightly lit streets, determined to reach the Rasa Sayang Hotel on the dot of eight o'clock. The last meeting would have all the marks of a pure business transaction: perfect punctuality, precision of words said, propriety of manner displayed.

She could see him now, walking quickly up to her while she stood in the hotel lobby facing him. His first words would be those he had prepared her for, in his last letter: "I love you. Will you be mine?" His overweening confidence would then suffer its first blow: "No." The single word answer was part of a reality he would never be able to see. But that would be his problem, not hers. "No, Jeremy, no." And she would go on, in fairness to him, to. explain the stand she was taking: "I want to tell you why I have come all the way this evening, to see you, even though my answer is 'No'. It is something I need to complete the healing process. You can have no idea how long it takes a woman, when she has been shattered from the inside, to recover. Perhaps she never does. Forgetting takes far too long. I never opened your letters because they would only prolong the pain of not forgetting. 1 could not destroy them, for that would have its own kind of pain. So I am returning them all to you now. With the last of the connections with you gone, I will be free at last. So it's no, Jeremy, no, and goodbye."

The rehearsal did have a calming effect. She saw her own words scrolling across her brain, and felt their mournfulness weighing on her heart. It was going to be dreadful, this last meeting, this most painful experience in her life, and she wanted it over quickly. She would, dry-eyed and calm-voiced, preside over the demise of her dream, then turn and walk away.

She turned on the car radio, for soft music to assist in the calming of her nerves, and heard part of an announcement, made in a tone of extreme gravity, containing the words 'Rasa Sayang Hotel'. She turned on the volume, and heard a repetition of the utterance, clearly part of an overall earlier announcement, so that it took her some time to understand what it meant: "... six o'clock this evening – police have cordoned off the area. Motorists, please avoid Heng Boon Road and Peterson Road. The rescuers have already brought out many of the dead and injured ... many feared buried in the rubble."

There followed a brief account of the history of the doomed hotel, one of the oldest in Singapore, but renovated a few years ago, to serve as a special hotel for honeymooners and bridal parties. A check had shown that the renovation work had not been in compliance with the regulations contained in the Buildings and Renovations Act. There would be a full police investigation. Meanwhile, the concern was to save those trapped in the rubble.

Li-ann, her face white, her lips dry, raced to the scene of the disaster. She would reproach herself later for her concern for only one person, as if others did not matter. Six o'clock. Would that have been the time for his shower, shave, rest, whatever, in readiness to meet her? Or could he have been outside the hotel then, like many lucky others, taking a stroll, doing some shopping? Perhaps he had suddenly decided to take a sentimental walk back to the Blue Paradise Café, across the road? Or was he already dead, buried under the rubble?

She parked her car in a car park some distance away, and was about to start walking to the scene of the tragedy when she stopped, returned to her car, opened it and took out the box of letters. She had no idea what she was going to do with them, except that, in some strange way, they would be a comforting presence in the growing despair that her last thoughts of their writer were such bitter ones. "I'm sorry," she could say to them, and hope that in the strange ways by which the dead could hear the living, Jeremy would know she bore no ill will against him after all.

Joining the large crowd of people who had gathered round to watch and were repeatedly pushed back by alert police where they pressed too close against the ropes and barriers set up, she gasped to see the dereliction of a place that four years ago, had been the scene of the happiest wedding party she had ever witnessed, of the moment of greatest happiness she had ever known. The four-storey hotel had collapsed into a huge mound of earth, bricks, stone, glass and metal, as if some bad-tempered child giant or god, tired of his toy, had dropped it to the ground and smashed it with his boots.

She heard screaming and crying from those trapped inside, and from those trapped outside, in their helplessness to save their loved ones. She saw a woman crying hysterically, held back by two people; she saw the rescuers pull out a child, covered with blood. There were photographers from the newspapers, urgently clicking away. Their pictures of a foot sticking out of a mound of bricks, of the injured laid out on stretchers, covered with blankets, and rushed to the ambulances, of a young man with his face in his bands, of a small group of people huddled together, saying prayers, would be splashed in the newspapers for days. Soon there would be the stories of heroic rescue, of a tragic last-minute decision by an elderly woman tourist to return to the hotel for a rest instead of continuing with the shopping, of a young seventeen-year-old bellhop who was in the third day of his job.

Where was Jeremy?

She stood, pale and shivering, in the darkness lit in patches by lamps and searchlights set up hurriedly, watching the scene of heartbreak, her mind and heart in such turmoil that she could not have uttered one coherent thought or expressed one coherent feeling. "Oh my god," she whispered to herself, "oh my god." She became aware of a numbness in her legs that was spreading slowly through her whole body. She felt a few drops of rainwater on her face and ignored them. At one point she thought she was going to faint. "Oh my god," she said again, and the words, empty in themselves, were yet her means to stay connected to the evening's horror unfolding before her eyes.

Someone came up and said, "No point waiting, miss. It's going to rain. Rescue operations might have to stop." He was clearly one of the officers who had been quickly mobilised for the operation, equally urgent, of taking care of those in the unspeakable agony of waiting for news. Her pale, stricken face must have struck him, for he said, very gently, "There's a café across the road. You could wait there if you like. The café owner has kindly agreed to keep it open all night, to provide shelter and hot drinks."

A thought, totally irrelevant to the tragedy at hand, strayed into her mind: Ten o'clock, the waitress had told them at their first meeting there, way back in 1980. We close at ten o'clock. Do you have any more orders?

She chose a spot, lit dimly by a nearby street lamp, which had a patch of grass she could sit on, and continued to look upon the scene of devastation and grief.

Tragedy has a softening power on even the hardest hearts. She had come with a cold determination to end everything with a grim finality. Her speech would have its own grand finale: "You know why I've come? I'll tell you. All our meetings on 29 February, stretching over so many years, have been yours, because you'd gone away happy, while I'd returned to my life, broken and humiliated. I want this last meeting to be mine. I want to walk away from it, not crying, but smiling with my head held high. I want the triumph of this last meeting to erase the pain of all the earlier meetings." She would then hand over the box of his letters which he could see in their unopened state, turn and walk away. Walking away – this time she would do it well.

Tragedy has no place for the grim hand of revenge. Li an began to sob and to say to herself, "I'm so sorry, I'm so sorry." There were kind people everywhere, scuttling about in the darkness, with flashlights, ready to dispense comfort and hot tea. A woman whose two sons were waiters in the hotel had fainted from exhaustion and was being carried to the Blue Paradise Café.

She was aware of her own exhaustion, and sat down on the patch of grass, putting the box of letters by her side. She took off the string, opened the box and looked at the letters inside. She looked at them a long time, and suddenly felt a compulsion to read them. The urge, beaten down for so long, now asserted itself powerfully and was actually directing her fingers, trembling and cold, to pull the letters out of the box and spread them on her lap as she sat on the grass. She picked one up at random, tore off the envelope and began reading it. When she finished, she took out another, and then another. They were not in the sequence in which he had sent them, so the stories they told were all scrambled together, providing no continuing narrative.

But each story was complete in itself, needing no link to the others to form one tale. For each was not so much a story as a simple assertion of truth and a pleading for that truth to be believed. "I am asking for something very big from you," he had said again and again in his letters. "To believe me. I need you to make a leap of faith, if you cannot make a leap of love. Perhaps they are the same."

Letter after letter yielded the plea: Please believe me. Please trust me.

In the dim light afforded by the nearby street lamp, she read, again and again, each letter, as the hours dragged by in the night. She looked up, and noticed that many of the people in the watching crowd had gone home. The rescue workers were still at work, their activity slowed down by the darkness which had descended, like an ominous pall, over the city. She heard the sounds of the machines of rescue, and of voices giving orders, voices responding to the orders. Once she thought she heard a moan that rose, swelled and filled the night.

Where is Jeremy?

Twenty Two

She thought mournfully, *it took a tragedy for me to read his letters, and it may be too late.* Or perhaps tragedy was necessary, coming in its own time, to soften her heart into giving truth a chance. Truth and love – there could not be one without the other; the heart demanded both, and suffered from the betrayal by either.

Again and again in his letters, he said, "Please believe me. This is the truth." In the end he had no other recourse than sheer persistence, in the simple conviction that something reiterated long enough and passionately enough, would enter even the most resistant heart.

In several letters, he narrated the events of that dreadful evening, four years ago, simply and plainly, unadorned by description of any feelings that attended them. No anger, no rancour, no bitterness. He wrote that he was ready to come to Singapore, on his own, for the important meeting on 29 February 1988, when almost at the last minute, his son insisted on being taken along, an insistence, he later found out from Dylan, that had come from Francine. Dylan had created a scene, crying and saying that he wanted Francine to go along too, to take care of him.

That was all the reference he made to the machinations of a

scheming woman who must have been bent on marrying him. He blamed himself for not telling Francine the truth about his feelings, fearing to cause pain or offence. "I have no excuse," he said. "These things don't come easily to me. I suppose I'm a coward." He blamed himself for his failure to tell her the truth when they had met in Singapore: "I was careless. I was thoughtless. I hope you will believe me when I say there was no intention to deceive you. It seemed so unimportant, so irrelevant to our meeting and I was so caught up in the joy of seeing you and being with you again, that it slipped my mind entirely." He felt compelled to add, "Francine is just Dylan's teacher to me. But I am very grateful to her for caring so much about my son."

There was a letter in which a name jumped up at her. "I kept thinking about this man called K.S." Li-ann noted that the year was 1989. So it must have been among his earliest letters. "You seemed to care so much about him, running to make those phone calls. I had never experienced this thing called jealousy before. But I suppose I felt it then, and confess to feeling it now. If you are in love with him, or are already married to him, would you please let me know? I will take a long walk in the woods, and come back, feeling no better. But please let me know."

The most distressed letter was written in late 1991: "Why haven't you replied? I both fear and long for a reply. The fear is for a reply that forbids any more letters. So no news is good news in my case, if you can call the desperate persistence of hope good news! Sometimes, I feel a dark despair."

One of the last letters, in January 1992, had a cheerful note. He wrote about the loved objects still in tender keeping: her note in 1980, the red thread of the fortune-teller, the lipstick for the joyful message. "I had a dream once," he wrote enthusiastically, "of you standing on Orchard Road, waving your hands with the lipstick message at me and shouting, 'Yes, yes! I love you too. Don't you see?'"

Li-ann noticed among the letters one she should have noticed earlier, because the handwriting on the envelope was different. The postmark showed the year 1990. She tore it open. There was a single sheet inside, and her eyes were drawn instantly to the signature at the end: 'Francine' in an angry flourish of elegant loops, leapt up at her. She read the words above it, expecting them to show the same angry energy. Instead, they were full of sweetness. "I must thank you from the bottom of my heart," Francine had written, "for the supreme kindness of opening my eyes to the real person that Jeremy is. For without that incident in Singapore in which you played such a major role, I would never have known and would have found out the truth too late. Jeremy is the most selfish person I have ever met. He is weak and obsessive. He has no sense of gratitude. I am lucky to have learnt the truth about him, thanks to you, and luckier to have met Pierre, who is the exact opposite. We are going to be married soon. I wish you all luck and happiness. And if one day you should have responsibility of Dylan, I hope you will give him the care and love that he needs."

In one short note, Francine had put a saving face on her disastrous attempt to hook a man, to take her revenge on him by painting him with her brush of malice, to mock the woman he loved, and finally to claim ultimate victory in her new happiness.

Li-ann crushed the letter into a little ball and threw it away. It could not be allowed to take its place with the other letters in the box.

Right now, in her confused and fevered state, the message

that ran through all his letters appeared in clusters of crazily dancing words in her mind, and as a turbulence of powerful feelings in her heart. In the days and months to follow, she would go through each and every letter carefully and absorb the message in the full ardour and simplicity of its every word.

Something made her get up quickly, put back the letters in the box and walk back to her original place by the cordoning rope, only a short distance from the rescue operations. The rescuers were still at work. She saw them move about in the darkness, lit up in patches, heard the urgent sounds of spades hitting rocks, of earth being shovelled up, the scream of an ambulance driving away.

She stood silently waiting by the rope, aware of an ache throughout her whole body, and a numbing chill in her hands.

She must have waited for hours. Her body ached so much that she sat down on the ground for a while, then got up again, to peer once more into the darkness, to follow with eyes of hope alternating with despair the activity of a small group of men pulling away rocks and pieces of timber with their bare hands. Then she turned, started, and stared. For she saw a stretcher being carried by two men, picking their way carefully through the rubble, to reach the waiting ambulances. Jeremy! She could recognise the still form on the stretcher. It was very dark, for the light was very dim here, but she could recognise him. Her heart gave such an immense leap that it almost knocked her to the ground.

"Miss, miss, you can't... Stop..." One of the officers in charge was trying to stop her as she broke through the cordon and ran towards the stretcher.

"Jeremy!" she shrieked.

"Miss, you can't." The officer restrained her, holding her

tightly by the arm. She began to struggle to break free, then broke out crying. She sobbed so hard that he felt sorry for her.

"Miss, I'm very sorry, but we have orders…"

She clutched his arm. "Please," she begged. "Please. I love him so much. Let me see him."

The officer relented, and allowed her to go up to where the men were still making their way carefully through the rubble. He followed her closely.

"Jeremy!" she called, as she approached. Now it was the turn of the stretcher bearers to stop her.

"You can't," they said, and turned to see the officer give the signal for permission. The officer said to Li-ann, "Only for a short while. Please. Don't get too close. We're only doing our duty."

The stretcher bearers were startled by the movements coming from the inert form on the stretcher. They had given him for dead, or thought, if he had any breath left in his crushed body, that he would never survive the ride to the hospital. But the man was stirring. He was stirring in response to the woman's call.

"Jeremy! Jeremy!"

The injured man was actually making an attempt to sit up. But he fell back, groaning in pain.

"Let's go," said the stretcher bearers, but the man stopped them. "Please," he begged, and they knew what he meant.

"All right," they said, in the concession that even stern duty must sometimes make to the heart. "Your wife can come with you to the hospital."

Li-ann hurried up, breathlessly. He was about to be lifted up into the ambulance when a new alertness of his body, a new brightness in his eyes approaching pure joy, startled his attendants into a pause. They followed the direction of his eyes, and saw that they were fixed on the woman who was now standing close by, or rather, on something written on her palms, turned outwards, waving wildly in the dim light. The woman, swaying her arms high up in the air, was beaming a message that made the attendants smile when they understood it. They saw the large letter 'O' on one palm and the equally large letter 'K' on the other, both bright red, like happy letters in a child's alphabet, and smiled at the ingenuity of love. Okay, the woman was saying with her lipstick, to encourage her injured husband or lover or boyfriend to give him the will to survive his injuries. Okay, you'll live after all.

Jeremy stared. He tried to raise himself again, as if to reach the bearer of the message of hope. The rapture in his eyes told his attendants that he couldn't go yet; the driver of the ambulance mustn't start his engine yet, for he had to drink in the full joy of that moment. The attendants smiled again and whispered something to each other, aware they were witnessing one of those moments of pure love and joy that can occur even in the midst of tragedy.

"Jeremy," said Li-ann, and now she was close by his side and bent over him. She put her face lightly on his and began crying.

"Okay, lady, you'd better come with him now. We've got to go. We can't wait any longer."

She stood by while they lifted him gently into the ambulance, then scrambled up herself He would be slipping in and out of consciousness, but right now, his joy broke through his pain, making him remarkably lucid. She held his hand in hers. When the red of the lipstick transferred to his palm, she lifted it up for him to see. He smiled, before slipping once more into unconsciousness. He would tell her later, in the hospital, when she was allowed to see him, that during the ride to the hospital, he had a dream and saw himself standing on Orchard Road that day waving his arms about with his message for her, and saw her running to join him, waving her reply. He would marvel at the vividness of the dream, and she would not have the heart to tell him that dreams never occurred during unconsciousness, only during sleep and the waking hours.

In the ambulance, she watched him close his eyes and held his hand more tightly in hers. She closed her eyes and breathed deeply, then held up the loved hand to lay against her cheek. She heard the sounds of traffic outside, and saw, to her great surprise as she looked out of the ambulance window, that the first rays of dawn were already lighting up the sky.

About the Author

Catherine Lim is internationally recognised as one of the leading figures in the world of Asia fiction. The prolific writer and commentator has penned more than 20 books across various genres—short stories, novels, reflective prose, poems and satirical pieces. Many of her works are studied in local and foreign schools and universities, and have been published in various languages in several countries.

Also by Catherine Lim

Fiction
Deadline for Love
The Howling Silence: Tales of the Dead and Their Return
A Shadow of a Shadow of a Dream
The Catherine Lim Collection
The Bondmaid
The Teardrop Story Woman
Following the Wrong God Home
The Song of Silver Frond
Miss Seetoh in the World

Non-Fiction
Roll Out the Champagne, Singapore!
A Watershed Election: Singapore's GE 2011
An Equal Joy